She'd imagined s... ny
times, and every her.

Before she knew what was happening, Carson
brought her fantasy to reality by dipping his head
and pressing his lips to hers. The champagne was
just strong enough to mute the voices in her head
that told her this was a bad idea. Instead, she gave
in to his kiss, pulling him closer.

He tasted like champagne and spearmint; his touch
gentle, yet firm. She could've stayed just like this
forever, but eventually, Carson pulled away.

His green eyes reflected sudden panic. Her emotions
came crashing back down to the ground with the
reality she saw there. She had just kissed her boss.
Her boss!

"Georgia, I…" he started, his voice trailing off. "I didn't
mean for that to happen."

With a quick shake of her head, she dismissed his
words and took a step back from him. "Don't worry
about it," she said. "Excitement and champagne will
make people do stupid things every time."

The problem was that it didn't feel stupid.

* * *

Saying Yes to the Boss is part of the Dynasties:
The Newports series: Passion and chaos
consume a Chicago real estate empire

Dear Reader,

When I was asked to participate in this series, I was told that my story would be the first. It made me a little nervous. What if my book was boring and no one read the rest of the series? What if I made a change that screwed up my fellow authors in later books and they all hated me? Let it never be said that I'm not a worrywart. I stress out about everything, as many authors do. But thankfully, there was little for me to be concerned about. This is a great story and it didn't require me to change things later in the series.

The Newport brothers are a force to be reckoned with, and I was very happy to have Carson's story. As the youngest, he's never really felt like he belongs. No one understands how that feels more than his public relations director, Georgia. As a foster child, she's never had a family of her own, but she's found something close with her coworkers at the Newport Corporation. She's made a great life and a career for herself and she isn't about to risk it, even for the attentions of her handsome and charming boss. That just spells disaster.

Carson isn't the kind that takes no for an answer, however! Once his lips touch Georgia's, there's no going back. That's where the fun begins. If you enjoy Carson and Georgia's story, tell me by visiting my website at www.andrealaurence.com, liking my fan page on Facebook or following me on Twitter. I'd love to hear from you!

Enjoy,

Andrea

ANDREA LAURENCE

———

SAYING YES TO THE BOSS

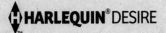

HARLEQUIN® DESIRE

If you purchased this book without a cover you should be aware
that this book is stolen property. It was reported as "unsold and
destroyed" to the publisher, and neither the author nor the
publisher has received any payment for this "stripped book."

Special thanks and acknowledgment are given
to Andrea Laurence for her contribution to the
Dynasties: The Newports miniseries.

Recycling programs
for this product may
not exist in your area

ISBN-13: 978-0-373-73471-9

Saying Yes to the Boss

Copyright © 2016 by Harlequin Books S.A.

All rights reserved. Except for use in any review, the reproduction or
utilization of this work in whole or in part in any form by any electronic,
mechanical or other means, now known or hereinafter invented, including
xerography, photocopying and recording, or in any information storage
or retrieval system, is forbidden without the written permission of the
publisher, Harlequin Enterprises Limited, 225 Duncan Mill Road,
Don Mills, Ontario M3B 3K9, Canada.

This is a work of fiction. Names, characters, places and incidents are
either the product of the author's imagination or are used fictitiously,
and any resemblance to actual persons, living or dead, business
establishments, events or locales is entirely coincidental.

This edition published by arrangement with Harlequin Books S.A.

For questions and comments about the quality of this book,
please contact us at CustomerService@Harlequin.com.

® and TM are trademarks of Harlequin Enterprises Limited or its
corporate affiliates. Trademarks indicated with ® are registered in the
United States Patent and Trademark Office, the Canadian Intellectual
Property Office and in other countries.

Printed in U.S.A.

R0445881869

Andrea Laurence is an award-winning author of contemporary romances filled with seduction and sass. She has been a lover of reading and writing stories since she was young and is thrilled to share her special blend of sensuality and dry, sarcastic humor with readers. A dedicated West Coast girl transplanted into the Deep South, she's working on her own happily-ever-after with her boyfriend and their collection of animals.

Books by Andrea Laurence

Harlequin Desire

Brides and Belles

Snowed In with Her Ex
Thirty Days to Win His Wife
One Week with the Best Man
A White Wedding Christmas

Secrets of Eden

Undeniable Demands
A Beauty Uncovered
Heir to Scandal
Her Secret Husband

Millionaires of Manhattan

What Lies Beneath
More Than He Expected
His Lover's Little Secret
The CEO's Unexpected Child

Dynasties: The Newports

Saying Yes to the Boss

Visit the Author Profile page at Harlequin.com, or andrealaurence.com, for more titles.

To My Fellow Newport Authors —

Kat, Sarah, Jules, Michelle and Charlene

Thanks for being so much fun to work with
on this series.

And to our editor, Charles—

You're awesome, as always. I'm still waiting
to see that infamous fanny pack.

One

"I found it."

Georgia Adams eyed Carson Newport from her position in his office doorway. He looked up from the paperwork on his desk, arched one golden eyebrow in curiosity and leaned back in his chair. "You found what?"

Georgia stifled a frown of disappointment. She'd imagined this moment differently. She was carrying a chilled bottle of champagne in her purse to celebrate her discovery. Not once in her imagination had he stared at her blankly.

How could he not know that she had found *it*? The Holy Grail of real estate. The very thing they'd been searching for, for months. "I found the spot where the Newport Corporation is going to be building the Cynthia Newport Memorial Hospital for Children."

That got his attention. Carson straightened up in his leather executive chair and pinned her with his gaze. "Are you serious?"

Georgia grinned. This was more like it. "As a heart attack."

"Come in." He waved her into his office. "Tell me all about it."

She shook her head and crooked her finger to beckon him. "I think I need to show you. Come on."

Carson didn't so much as look at his calendar for conflicts before he leaped from his chair. Finding the land for their next real estate development project had been *that* hard and *that* important. There wasn't a lot of space in Chicago to do what they wanted. At least, not at a price that made any kind of financial sense.

He moved swiftly around his massive mahogany desk, buttoning the black suit coat he was wearing as he joined her in the doorway. "Lead on, Miss Adams."

Georgia spun on her heel and headed for the elevators. "We're taking your car," she reminded him as she hit the down button.

He leaned his palm against the wall and looked down at her. "You know, Georgia, you're the director of public relations at a Fortune 500 company. I think I pay you enough to get a car. I pay you enough to get a really nice car. There's even a reserved spot in the garage for you that sits open every day."

Georgia just shrugged. She didn't want the responsibility of a car. In truth, she didn't need one. Her apartment was a block away from the "L." Chicago's elevated train was efficient and cheap, and that's how she liked things. She'd never owned a car before. Public transportation was all she'd ever really known. To some people who grew up the way she had, finally getting their own car would be a milestone that showed they had made something of themselves. To her, it was an unnecessary expense. She never knew when she might need that money for something else.

"You look like a Jaguar girl to me." Carson continued to ponder aloud as they stepped out of the elevator to the employee parking deck. "Graceful, attractive and just a little bit naughty."

Georgia stopped beside Carson's pearl-white Range Rover. She brushed her loose platinum-blond hair over her shoulder and planted a hand on her hip. "Mr. Newport, am I going to have to report you to human resources?" she asked with a smile that took the teeth out of the threat.

Carson winced as he opened the door for her to get inside. "It was just a compliment. Please don't make me go to the second floor. Our HR director reminds me of my third-grade teacher. She was always mean to me."

"Were you poorly behaved?" Georgia challenged him.

Carson grinned, showcasing his bright smile. His

sea-green eyes twinkled mischievously. "Maybe," he admitted before slamming the door.

She took the next ten seconds alone to take a deep breath. Being around Carson Newport was hard on Georgia's nerves. Not because he was a difficult boss—he was anything but. That was part of the problem. He was handsome, charming, smart and a miserable flirt. All the Newport brothers were that way, but only Carson made Georgia's heart race. His flattering banter was harmless. She knew that. He'd never so much as touched her in the year she'd worked for his company.

That didn't mean she didn't secretly want him to. It was a stupid fantasy, one that kept her up nights as she imagined his hands running over her bare skin. But it had to stay a fantasy. She'd worked damn hard to get into a good college and climb the corporate ladder. Landing this job at the Newport Corporation was a dream come true. She'd found a family among her coworkers here. She was good at her job. Everything had turned out just as she'd hoped. Georgia wasn't about to risk that just because she had the hots for her boss.

Carson climbed in the car and they headed out. It took about a half hour to negotiate downtown traffic and get out to the site she'd found. Once there, he pulled his Range Rover off the road and onto a patch of grass and gravel. They both got out of the car and walked a couple hundred yards into a large empty field.

If she'd known she was coming out here today before she left the house, she would've opted for a more practical outfit than a pencil skirt and heels, but she didn't get the tip on the land until she got into the office. Fortunately it hadn't rained for a while, so the ground was firm and dry. It really was an ideal plot of land. The property was fairly level without many trees that would need to be cleared. One side butted up to an inlet of Lake Michigan and another to a waterfront park.

"So…" Georgia said at last. The anticipation was killing her. She didn't know how they could find anything better than this. The property had been tied up in probate for years and the family had just now decided to sell it, or it would've long ago been turned into a shopping center or condos. If Carson didn't like it, not only was she back to the drawing board, but she also had a really expensive bottle of champagne in her purse for no reason at all. "What do you think?"

She watched Carson survey the property with his back to her for a few minutes. When he finally faced her, his winning grin was broader than ever. "It's amazing. Perfect."

Carson walked across the empty field with his hands shoved into his pants pockets. There was a casual air about him that belied how intense he could be in business affairs. Georgia had seen more than one person underestimate the youngest Newport and regret it.

"How did you ever find out about this place?"

"I know a guy," Georgia said with a smile. She'd sent out quiet feelers several weeks ago and hadn't heard anything back until today. An acquaintance from college had told her about the land. It wasn't publicly for sale, at least not yet. She'd spoken to the owners and they were entertaining bids on the whisper listing through the end of next week. She got the idea they wanted to move quickly and with as little hassle as possible. If they didn't get an offer they liked by then, they'd announce the sale. If the Newport Corporation moved fast, they could avoid the sale becoming public and competitors driving up the price of the land.

Carson turned back to her. "You know a guy? I love it."

"Shall we buy it?" Georgia asked. "We don't have a lot of time to decide. Someone will snatch it up, I'm certain."

"Yes, I think we should buy it and quickly. Let's not even wait for my brothers' opinions. Graham and Brooks will think it's great."

Georgia smiled and slipped her purse off her shoulder. The large bag could've easily accommodated enough stuff for a weekend vacation, but it was the purse that she carried every day. Anything she could ever possibly need was in that bag. Today that included an insulated bag with chilled champagne and cups. "I think this is cause for celebration," she said as she pulled out the bottle.

"You're like Mary Poppins with that thing," Carson said with a chuckle as he leaned close to peer into the abyss of her handbag. "What else do you have in there?"

Reaching back inside, Georgia pulled out two red plastic cups. "They're not lead crystal, but they'll do."

"That's perfect. I've done all my best celebrating with Solo cups." Carson took the champagne bottle and opened it. He let the cork fly across the field and then poured them both a healthy-size glass.

"To the new Cynthia Newport Memorial Hospital for Children!" Carson said, holding up his glass.

"To finally seeing your mother's dream realized!" Georgia added.

As they both took a sip, Georgia noticed the faraway look of sadness in Carson's eyes. It had been only about two months since his mother's sudden death from an aneurysm. They'd had no warning at all. She was there, and then she was gone. Their mother was all they had for family. The brothers had taken it all very hard, but Carson especially. He decided he wanted to build a children's hospital in her honor, since she'd done so much charity work with sick kids in her later years.

"I really can't believe we're making this happen." Setting down his cup, Carson wrapped Georgia in his arms and spun her around.

"Carson!" Georgia squealed and clung to his neck, but that only made him spin faster.

When he finally set her back on the ground, both of them were giggling and giddy from drinking the champagne on empty stomachs. Georgia stumbled dizzily against his chest and held to his shoulders until the world stopped moving around her.

"Thank you for finding this," he said.

"I'm happy to. I know it's important to you," she said, noting he still had his arms around her waist. Carson was the leanest of the three brothers, but his grip on her told of hard muscles hidden beneath his expensive suit.

In that moment, the giggles ceased and they were staring intently into each other's eyes. Carson's full lips were only inches from hers. She could feel his warm breath brushing over her skin. She'd imagined standing like this with him so many times, and every one of those times, he'd kissed her.

Before she knew what was happening, Carson brought her fantasy to reality by dipping his head and pressing his lips to hers. The champagne was just strong enough to mute the voices in her head that told her this was a bad idea. Instead she gave in to his kiss, pulling him closer.

He tasted like champagne and spearmint. His

touch was gentle yet firm. She could've stayed just like this forever, but eventually, Carson pulled back from the kiss.

For a moment, Georgia felt light-headed. She didn't know if it was his kiss or the champagne, but she felt as though she would lift right off the ground if she let go. Then she looked up at him.

His green eyes reflected sudden panic. Her emotions came crashing back down to the ground with the reality she saw there. She had just kissed her boss. Her boss! And despite the fact that he had initiated it, he looked just as horrified by the idea.

"Georgia, I…" he started, his voice trailing off. "I didn't mean for that to happen."

With a quick shake of her head, she dismissed his words and took a step back from him. "Don't worry about it," she said. "Excitement and champagne will make people do stupid things every time."

The problem was that it didn't feel stupid. It had felt amazing. Better than any fantasy she'd ever had about Carson. But that didn't make it a good idea.

"I hope this won't make things awkward between us. I'd hate for my thoughtlessness to ruin our working relationship."

"It's fine, Carson. Please. Things happen when you work closely with someone. Besides that," she admitted reluctantly, "I wasn't exactly fighting you off."

"Georgia?"

She'd avoided his gaze once their lips parted and she saw his inevitable regret, but the pleading, husky sound of his voice as he said her name made her look back at him. The regret was gone and there was a fire in his eyes now as he looked at her. His jaw was tight. With an expression like that, she would say he desired her, but that couldn't possibly be right. That kiss was a mistake and they both knew it. Right? "Yes?"

"I—"

A hard buzz against Georgia's breast startled her. At the same time, a chirp sounded from Carson's suit pocket, interrupting what he was about to say. It was their office phones.

Georgia swallowed her disappointment, turned her back to him and reached into her blouse to retrieve her phone. She always kept it on silent, tucked away in her shirt so she would know when she got a call without interrupting business. When she looked down, the message on the screen nearly devastated her.

"Sutton Winchester has announced plans to build luxury waterfront condos here," Carson said.

Georgia clicked on the link to the news article his administrative assistant, Rebecca, had sent them both. She'd left the information on the property with Rebecca in case Brooks or Graham came in and asked where they were. Instead she'd used it to uncover their competition. The story was accompanied by an image of the fancy development they planned to build on the spot where they were standing. The article noted that Sutton's offer on the land hadn't been accepted yet, but he was confident that it would be, and he was rallying support for the project. Below the artist's rendering of the buildings was a picture of Sutton Winchester.

Georgia had no doubt Sutton must have been able to charm any woman he wanted when he was a younger man. He had quite the reputation where women were concerned even now, despite his age and longtime marriage to Celeste Van Houten. Georgia could see why. His light brown hair was mostly gray now and wrinkles lined his face, but his green eyes were still bright, and his dimpled smile exuded confidence. Fortunately Georgia knew to stay far away from the likes of Winchester. He was an underhanded bastard in business dealings. He bribed, seduced and lied to get his way, screwing over the Newport Corporation on more than one occasion and putting a handful of other companies out of business entirely.

Georgia let her phone drop to her side and turned back to face Carson. Their kiss faded into her distant memory as she focused on their next steps.

There was a steely determination set into his expression when he looked at her. "We need to move quickly. I can't—*I won't*—let that bastard Sutton steal this out from under us."

"There's no way in hell you can let Winchester have our land," Graham complained.

Carson reached over the back of his leather sofa, handed his older brother a bowl of hot buttered popcorn and rolled his eyes. He was hoping they wouldn't spend tonight talking about this, but it was clear Graham wasn't going to let it go. "You think I don't know that?"

"Has our offer gone in yet?" Graham's twin, Brooks, asked. The older brothers were identical, each a good two inches taller than Carson with shaggy blond hair and aqua eyes. It was easy for Carson to tell his brothers apart, though. Brooks's brow was always furrowed with concern and thought. He had that exact expression now as he tried to balance the three bottles of microbrew that he brought with him from the kitchen.

Carson nodded and went back through his dining room to the kitchen to grab a bag of M&M'S and a box of Twizzlers off the quartz bar. "We called and submitted the offer while we were still standing in the field. The seller's attorney was mum about other offers they'd received, including Winchester's. There's no way to know if what we've submitted is on par with the others, so all we can do is wait and see if they come back with a counteroffer before they make a final decision."

Carson settled on the couch beside his brothers. "Now, can we please let this unpleasant conversation drop so we can enjoy *The Maltese Falcon* in peace?"

"Fine," Graham muttered and shoved a handful of popcorn into his mouth.

It was the first Thursday of the month, and that meant it was movie night in the Newport family. Since they were small, they'd gathered on the couch with their mother and Gerty to watch old black-and-white movies on AMC. Gerty, a widow, had worked with their mother at a café where they waitressed together before Carson was born. When Gerty retired, she'd invited Cynthia and her boys to live with her. The apartment their mother could afford was tiny and she had three growing boys who needed room to roam. Gerty didn't like being in her big house all alone and welcomed the family.

She wasn't blood, but Gerty had been the only family they had besides each other. For reasons their mother had never wanted to discuss, their father and the rest of their family were out of the picture. As Carson and his brothers got older and pushed, Cynthia had told them only that their father was abusive and she ran away to protect them all. They were better off without him in their lives, she insisted, and she made them promise not to seek him out.

For a long time, the boys had been saddened but content with that answer. They wouldn't want to hurt their mother by seeking out a dangerous man who would only make them regret it. Besides, they had their spunky pseudo grandmother Gerty and their mother. They didn't need anyone else.

Then they lost Gerty to cancer when they were in high school. She'd left them enough money to go to college and make something of themselves. Carson and his brothers had done just that, starting the Newport Corporation and becoming wealthier than they ever imagined by developing real estate in Chicago. They couldn't have done it without Gerty, so they honored her memory by drinking beer and watching the old favorites once a month.

"Double the offer," Graham insisted as he picked up the television remote and started the film.

"We can't afford that," Brooks argued, ever the voice of reason between the twins. Without him, Graham would've gotten himself into trouble with some crazy scheme long before now.

"We can find the money somewhere," Graham said, pausing the movie before it had even begun.

Carson sighed. He knew better than to think Graham would simply shut up about it. When he got an idea in his head, he wouldn't let it go. He was like a bulldog with a bone, which made him a great attorney, but a pain as a brother. Graham was the corporate attorney for the Newport Corporation, although he spent most of his time working at his law firm, Mayer, Mayer and Newport. Brooks was their chief operations officer but spent most days working remotely from his mansion on Lake Michigan. Carson was the CEO, running the company they'd started together, but that didn't stop his brothers from putting their two cents into every decision he made.

"Sure thing," Carson agreed. "We can start by firing our attorney and making him return his corporate car."

"Hey!" Graham complained. He shoved a sharp elbow into Carson's ribs.

Carson returned the elbow, making his brother howl and scramble to the far side of the couch. He was used to the physical and mental bullying that being the younger brother entailed, but he'd learned to fight back a long time ago. Now that they were in their thirties, it hadn't changed much. "You said to find the money. You didn't say where. Now, will you let it go so we can watch the movie?"

Graham scowled and picked up his beer from the coffee table. "Fine."

Brooks grabbed the remote from Graham and hit the play button. As the opening credits were still playing, Graham studied his bottle and said, "You know, Gerty would whup our asses for drinking this highbrow beer."

This time, Carson snorted aloud. He was right. Gerty preferred to watch her movies with a plain Hershey's bar and a can of classic Budweiser. If she'd still been alive, she'd have given them a hard time over their fancy new lives, including the small-batch artisanal brew they bought downtown.

"I miss Gerty," Brooks said, pausing the movie

just as the grainy black-and-white images of San Francisco came onto the screen.

"I miss Mom," Carson added.

The three brothers sat together in silence for a moment, acknowledging everything that they'd lost. Their mother's death had been so sudden, and their lives so busy, that they'd hardly had the time to sit and let the reality of her death hit them. They were alone now, except for each other. It was a sad thought, one Carson had tried to avoid. It sent his mind spiraling down into rabbit holes.

"When are we going to clean out her house?" Graham asked.

That was a task they'd also avoided. They'd had their mother's housekeeper throw away all the perishables and close the house up until they were able to deal with her things. Eight weeks had gone by and none of them had even set foot in their mother's home.

Brooks sighed. "We have to do it eventually. We can't leave her house sitting there like some kind of old shrine."

"I'll do it," Carson volunteered. The words slipped out so suddenly he surprised even himself. "Just let me take care of this land deal first. I have a feeling I'll have my hands full with Sutton for a while."

"Are you sure?" Brooks looked at him with his blond brows furrowed in concern. "You don't have to do it by yourself."

Carson shook his head. "You two don't have time.

Besides, I want to. Maybe being around her things will make me feel less…"

"Alone?"

He turned and looked at Brooks. "Maybe."

"Do you think…" Graham began, then hesitated. "Do you think we might find something about our father among her things?"

Carson had wondered the same thing several times, but hadn't allowed himself to speak the words out loud. "Mom wouldn't want us to find him."

"Mom doesn't get a vote anymore," Brooks argued. "Our father might be the royal bastard she always told us he was, but he's not the only one out there we might find. We might have siblings, cousins, grandparents… It's possible that we have a whole family out there that would be worth the effort to track down. Don't you want to know where we come from? We would finally be able to fill out our family tree. I know Mom tried to keep us from finding out the truth, but with her gone, I don't think she'd want us to feel as isolated as we do."

"We can at least try," Graham added. "If we find something we can use, great. If not, well, at least we can say we tried. It might be a stupid move that we'll regret, but at least we'll finally know for ourselves, right?"

His brothers were right. Carson knew it. They all felt a sense of not belonging. Finding where they came from, even if they didn't get the happy fam-

ily reunion they all secretly hoped for, would give
them closure. They'd always wonder if they didn't
find out the truth. Since their parents hadn't married and his name was left off their birth certificates,
cleaning out their mother's house might be the only
chance they had to uncover a clue. After that, their
only leads would be in the landfill.

"I'll keep my eyes open, okay?" Carson finally
agreed. "If I find something we can use, I'll let you
know."

The brothers nodded in agreement, and Brooks
picked up the remote again to start the movie for the
third and final time.

Two

"Mr. Newport? Miss Adams is here to see you, sir."

Carson reached out to his phone and hit the button to respond to Rebecca. "Please send her in."

The door to his office opened a minute later and Georgia stepped inside. Her platinum-blond hair was pulled back into a bun today, highlighting her high cheekbones and sharp chin. She was wearing a pewter pantsuit that very nearly matched the color of her steely gray eyes.

Carson had tried not to pay that much attention to how Georgia looked most days, but he usually failed. She was a fashionable woman who knew exactly what she should wear to highlight her outrageous curves. As her boss, he shouldn't notice she was built like a brick house. He shouldn't care that she wore a shiny lip gloss that made her pouty bottom lip call out to him.

And yet he couldn't stop himself. Kissing her in the field the other day had made it that much harder. Now he knew how those curves felt beneath his palms and that the lip gloss she wore was strawberry flavored. The feeling was ten times worse than it ever was before, and if there was a time he needed to focus on work and not on how badly he wanted his director of public relations, it was now.

"Any word?" she asked as she came across the room and settled into his guest chair.

"I spoke with the sellers directly this morning. They've still not made a decision. I told them to give us the chance to counter their offer before they choose someone else. That doesn't mean that Winchester won't do the same thing, bidding us up to well outside our top price."

"I hate this waiting game," Georgia said.

Carson sat back in his leather executive chair and brought his fingertips pensively to his lips. "Me, too. What other avenues can we pursue while we wait?"

"Well," Georgia began as she lifted her tablet and started tapping on the screen. "First, I think we should try talking to Winchester."

Carson put his coffee mug back down on his desk, happy he hadn't had a mouthful of steaming hot liquid to spit out when she made her suggestion. "Talk to Winchester? Are you serious?"

Georgia shrugged. "Why not? Surely the man can be reasoned with. This project is to help sick children. How could he possibly be against sick children?"

Carson chuckled and shook his head. "You obviously haven't met the *son of a bitch* yet. Did you know he refers to himself as the King of Chicago? A man with that kind of ego isn't going to back down for anything. Contacting him will just tip him off to the fact that we're his competition. He'll drive up the price just to watch us squirm."

"You don't think he already knows?" Georgia asked. "If we know he's bid, I'm sure he's got enough spies to know we have, as well. What he may not know is what we plan to do with the land. That might make a difference and get him to back down."

Carson put his elbows on his desk, leaned forward and gave her a wry smile. "You really are an optimist, aren't you?"

An odd expression came across her face, her brows pinching together in thought. "I guess you could say that. Sometimes there's nowhere to go but up," she responded cryptically.

He wasn't quite sure what to say to that, but he knew she was right. It couldn't hurt to call up Sutton and talk to him man-to-man. Winchester was old-school. It was possible he'd appreciate Carson manning up and calling him. It was also possible it wouldn't help, but at least he could say he'd tried to reason with him.

"Okay, you win," he said. "I'll call him, but don't get your hopes up."

Turning to his computer, he looked up Sutton's number and dialed the phone. All the while, Georgia watched him with a mix of excitement and anxiety on her face. Carson was pretty certain it would be replaced with disappointment soon enough. He didn't want to see those full lips turned down into a frown, but it probably couldn't be helped where Sutton was concerned.

A perky-sounding woman answered the phone. "Elite Industries, Mr. Winchester's office. How may I assist you?"

"Yes, this is Carson Newport. I'd like to speak with Sutton, please."

"Hold please, Mr. Newport."

An irritating instrumental music track started playing when Carson was put on hold. He tapped his fingers on the desk to the anxious rhythm in his mind as he waited. It took nearly two minutes for anyone to pick up the line again.

There was a short, muffled string of coughs. "Carson Newport," a man's voice barked into the phone. It was a deep, gravelly sound, laced with a cockiness that Carson didn't care for. "I wasn't expecting a call from you today. Tell me, what can the King of Chicago do for the Newport Corporation?"

Sit on it and rotate was the first thought that came to mind, but Carson swallowed the words. "Good afternoon, Sutton. I'm calling today to talk to you about the lakeside project you announced a few days ago."

"Won't it be splendid? Best waterfront views for miles. I've already got a list of potential buyers lined up for the best units. Are you interested in one, Carson? I'll give you the sweetest corner unit I've got. Wall-to-wall windows overlooking Lake Michigan."

Carson gritted his teeth. "That's a very kind offer, Sutton, but I'm not looking for a place to live. I'm actually looking for a place to build a new children's hospital."

There was a moment of silence on the line. "That's a very noble project," Sutton said, refusing to acknowledge what Carson was after.

"I agree. I think the Cynthia Newport Memorial Hospital for Children will be an asset to the community and a testimony to my mother's work with kids."

There was a longer silence on the line this time. Unsure of what was going through Sutton's mind, he went on. "The problem is that we were looking at the same property you've identified for those condos and put in our own bid around the time that you did."

"That's a shame."

Carson was really getting annoyed with Sutton's vagueness. He wasn't about to make it easier on Carson. He was going to make him ask for it. Beg for him to withdraw the offer. "I'm calling because I was hoping I could convince you to set the condo project aside and let us have the land to build the hospital."

"I'm afraid I can't do that, Carson. I've already got way too much money invested in this project."

"Sutton, I—"

"How about this?" Sutton interrupted. "How about tomorrow about three or so, you send that pretty little PR director of yours over here. I'll discuss it with her and see if we can't come to some kind of arrangement."

Carson looked down and realized his hand was clenched into a tight fist as though he could punch the old man through the phone line. He consciously unclenched and stretched his fingers, noticing Georgia's curious expression as she watched him across the desk.

"What is it?" she mouthed silently.

He could only shake his head and hold up a finger for her to wait. "That's not really her sandbox, Sutton."

"I don't care," Sutton snapped. "She will come here tomorrow at three or the discussion is over. You and your sick kids can find somewhere else to convalesce."

Before Carson could respond, the line went dead. He studied the phone in his hand a moment before setting it gently onto the cradle. He was a little shell-shocked from the conversation and needed a few moments to gather his thoughts.

"What did he say?"

"No," he said. Carson wasn't about to tell her about Sutton's demands. That guy had a reputation when it came to young and beautiful women. Carson wouldn't let any females in his social circle even get close to Winchester, especially not Georgia. He felt protective of her, even though he had no real claim to her. "I told you he wouldn't budge."

"He said a hell of a lot more than no," Georgia pointed out. "What did he say? Tell me."

Carson sighed. He sat back in his chair and ran his fingers through his blond waves. "It doesn't matter what he said, Georgia. The point is that he isn't going to back down."

Georgia arched one delicate brow and leaned forward. "Tell me, or heaven help me, I'll march down this hallway and tell your brother Sutton gave you an out but you refused to take it."

He immediately straightened up in his chair. "What is this, elementary school?"

She only shrugged and sat back, casually crossing her shapely legs. She couldn't have been over five-five, but sometimes Carson was certain that at least four feet of her was leg. He'd given a lot of thought to how they'd feel wrapped around his waist.

"Carson!"

He snapped out of his mental reverie and flung

his arm up in defeat. "Okay. He wants to meet with you." He spat out the words with disgust.

"With *me*? That doesn't make any sense."

Carson could only shake his head. "It makes perfect sense when we're talking about Sutton Winchester. He very specifically requested you and said he wouldn't speak to anyone else. I'm pretty sure he's interested in more than just talking to you, Georgia."

Georgia's lips formed a small O of surprise. "Wow," she said at last.

"I can't send you over there into that wolf den. Odds are that in the end, it won't make any difference. We just need to increase our offer and hope it's enough."

"No."

Carson frowned. "What do you mean, no?"

"I want to go. He's asked for me, so maybe I'm the one who can sway his decision."

"I can't risk it, Georgia. If that guy so much as lays a finger on you, I'll never forgive myself."

Georgia's lips curled into a wicked grin, highlighting today's dark burgundy lipstick. "I'm no debutante, Carson. I may have nice clothes and a good education now, but there was a time where I had to fight for survival each and every day. I can hold my own. If he gets inappropriate, I'll give him a good dose of pepper spray."

Now it was Carson's turn to look shocked. He envisioned Sutton Winchester—the King of Chicago—

rolling around on the ground as he screamed and clawed at his eyes. But he'd love to hear her tell him about it.

He also couldn't forget that he'd promised his brothers that he would make this hospital project happen. Whether he liked it or not, he needed to do whatever it took, even if it meant sending Georgia right into that bastard's clutches.

"Okay, you can go," he said at last. "On one condition. You take Big Ron with you." The head of security at the Newport Corporation was a former Olympic heavy lifter. He'd once told Carson he slapped a man across the face and accidently broke his jaw. He could snap Sutton like a twig, if necessary.

Georgia considered his stipulations for a moment and then nodded. "Okay. But he stays outside the office with the secretary unless I call him."

"May I offer you something to drink?"

"No, thank you," Georgia replied. Sitting in the guest chair across from Sutton Winchester's ostentatious oak desk, she couldn't help but fiddle with the collar of her shirt. After Carson's warnings yesterday, she'd chosen a pantsuit instead of a skirt and buttoned her blouse up to her throat.

It had been a long time since she'd dressed that way. Probably not since she lived with Mrs. Anderson. She'd been a religious fanatic and swore up and down that any inch of skin Georgia showed would tempt a good man into sin. Truth be told, once Georgia blossomed into her full figure, there wasn't anything a turtleneck would do to hide it.

Even now, she could feel Sutton's eyes rake across her body. The July heat in Chicago was absolutely miserable, but at the moment she was wishing she'd worn a heavy down coat.

Sutton poured himself a drink and settled back into his chair. Georgia noticed that the man in front of her bore little resemblance to the press picture she'd seen in the paper the other day. He was still a tall and relatively handsome man, but the green eyes watching her had a dull look. It was made more obvious by the bags under them and the wrinkles lining his brow. He looked ten years older than she'd expected, even with his wide grin and trademark dimples.

"So, Miss Adams, is it?" he asked before scooting up to the desk.

"Yes."

Sutton nodded and leaned forward to close some of the space between them. "I bet you're wondering why I asked you here today."

"Actually, yes. I'm not really the most qualified person to explain the plans the Newport Corporation has for the hospital, but I'll do the best I can. The current children's hospital is a dinosaur with outdated equipment and too few rooms and staff to provide for the number of children that need treatment. The plans we have for the new hospital will include state-of-the-art—"

Sutton held up his hand to silence her. "Actually, Miss Adams, you can stop there. To be honest, I didn't invite you here to talk about the land deal."

Georgia's brows went up in surprise. Carson had been right. She should've known better than to fall into this trap. Holding her purse tightly in her lap, she slipped one hand inside and wrapped her fingers around her trusty pepper spray. "May I ask why you did ask me here, Mr. Winchester?"

"Please, call me Sutton," he said with a smile that should've charmed her but immediately put Georgia on edge. In her years of foster care, she'd become a very good judge of character, and it took only a few minutes for her to know that she had to tread very carefully with this man.

"I saw you recently on the news speaking about the Newport Corporation's sponsorship of a charity fun run. I was impressed by you. Impressed enough that I had my people look into more of your work. You have a remarkable résumé for someone of your age."

Georgia tried not to squirm under his praise. She was very proud of how far she'd come in life. She'd worked damn hard to keep herself from becoming another sad statistic of the failing foster care system. Landing the job at Newport Corporation was the culmination of everything she had worked for. But she didn't like hearing it from Sutton's lips. Perhaps it was how he was looking at her as he said it.

"My director of public relations has recently retired. I haven't had a single applicant that could beat you out for the job."

Georgia straightened up in her seat and put on a flattered smile. "Luckily for them, I already have a job."

Sutton thoughtfully stroked his chin. "Yes, you do. But I think you can do better."

Her breath caught in her throat as Sutton pushed up from his chair and rounded the desk. He stopped just in front of her and leaned back on the edge. The hem of his pants brushed her ankle as he stretched out, causing her to tuck her legs up under the chair and out of his reach.

"What are you suggesting, Mr. Winchester?"

"I'm suggesting you come work for me, Georgia."

That wasn't going to happen. She didn't care for his cutthroat business practices. She wouldn't feel good about working for him. "And why would I do that?"

"Well," Sutton chuckled, "to start, it's the natural progression of your career. Everyone wants to work for the best, and Elite Industries is the best. Of course, there is also a generous benefits and compensation package. We offer an in-house day care, a fitness center and a month of vacation to start, plus telecommuting at least one day a week."

It sounded nice. *If* she was looking. And she wasn't.

"And then there's the signing bonus."

Georgia decided to bite. She'd done her fair share of market research to see if her earnings were on par with her peers'. If Elite Industries really was the step up he claimed it was, there should be some solid numbers behind that offer. "How much are we talking?"

"A million."

Her eyes widened as she struggled to choke down her shock. That was not at all what she was anticipating. A million dollar–signing bonus? What the hell kind of *salary* was he offering with a signing bonus like that? "That's very g-generous," she stuttered. "What's the catch?"

Sutton narrowed his green gaze at her and smiled wide. "Smart girl. Nothing is free in this world, as you are well aware, I'm sure. That said, I don't like to think of it as a catch. More as a…retainer for our mutually beneficial arrangement. You see, I'd like you to become more than just an employee to me, Georgia."

He said the words as casually as if he'd offered her a drink. It took Georgia a minute even to be certain she'd heard what she thought she did. Was he asking her to be his mistress? Carson had warned her that Sutton was a lech, but she'd never expected to be offered the opportunity to service him sexually as though it were another job opening at the company. Had his mistress retired, too?

"I'm flattered, Mr. Winchester. Really, I am. But I'm going to have to pass. On everything," she added with a pointed tone.

A flicker of disappointment danced over Sutton's worn face and then vanished just as quickly. "You don't have to decide now," he insisted. "It's a big decision. Go home and ponder what kind of opportunity I'm offering. Think about what you can do with a million dollars. When you change your mind, I'll be waiting."

Georgia wasn't going to change her mind. Not even for a million dollars. Even if Sutton wasn't old enough to be her father, he really wasn't her type. Thirty years ago, he might have attracted her at first sight, but his personality would've sunk that ship before it could sail. No amount of money or charisma would've changed that.

And even if Sutton was the most handsome, virtuous man she'd ever met, Georgia would still not be his employee. It was bad enough she'd gotten wrapped up in the moment and kissed Carson at the build site. She'd crossed the line with her boss and had regretted it ever since. Well, at least she regretted most of it. Kissing Carson had been amazing. She wanted more of him, and yet she was determined not to let that happen. Sleeping with the boss was bad news. And cliché. She refused to be cliché. She also refused to ruin the good thing she had going at the Newport Corporation.

Inappropriate relations in the workplace just led to awkwardness. Georgia was dedicated to doing her best work every day. She couldn't do that with Carson walking around, reminding her of what they did or didn't do. Things always got weird. It was bad enough she fantasized about him. Acting on it was another matter. Sutton had been a welcome distraction from what happened that day, but once the land deal was finalized, they'd both have to face what they'd done.

"I will think it over, Mr. Winchester, but my answer isn't going to change. Now, what about the children's hospital?"

Sutton sighed and crossed his arms over his chest. "My answer hasn't changed, either. We'll battle it out fair and square with the property owner and let the best—or at least the richest—man win. Unless, of course, you'd like to reconsider my offer… If you change your mind, then perhaps I might change mine, as well."

This was even worse than she'd thought. Now he was trying to twist her arm by using such a noble cause against her. What was she willing to do for sick children? A lot. But not that. She grew up with almost nothing, but she'd managed to hang on to her principles.

There was nothing else she could say, so Georgia stood up and slung her purse over her shoulder. "I guess we're done here," she said.

Sutton reached out to take her hand. He shook it for a moment, then held it longer than necessary. He ran his thumb over the back of her hand, sending a shiver of revulsion down her spine. "Consider my offer, Georgia. There are a lot of parents with sick children out there that would be willing to do anything to save their child. In the end, it isn't much of a sacrifice to help so many, is it?"

Georgia tugged her hand from his and rubbed the palm over her slacks to wipe him away from her skin. "Good afternoon, Mr. Winchester."

Three

"He *what*?"

Carson very rarely lost his temper in the office, but he could tell by Georgia's startled cringe that he'd just shouted loud enough for the people in Accounting to hear him. "I'm sorry," he said more softly. "Just please tell me I didn't hear you right."

She didn't need to answer him. He could tell by the distant look in her eye and her awkward, hunched posture with her arms crossed protectively over her chest that he'd heard her correctly. He'd always known Sutton was a bastard, but this time he'd gone too far.

"Don't make me say it again, Carson," she said softly.

He fought the protective urge to wrap his arms around her and tell her it would be okay. After the day she'd had, she probably didn't want a man touching her. Even him. Considering how quickly she'd backpedaled from their kiss the other day, she probably didn't want Carson touching her, ever.

Looking around his office, he decided maybe they needed a change of scene for this conversation. "Buy you a drink?" he asked.

Georgia looked down at her watch and sighed. "I'm not going to get any work done, so why not?"

It wasn't an enthusiastic response, but he didn't expect one given that she'd just come here straight from Sutton's office. He grabbed his phone and escorted her to the elevator. They exited the building and crossed the street, heading down the block to an Irish pub where Carson and his brothers had spent a good bit of their time and money over the years.

Since the official business day hadn't yet come to an end, the bar wasn't crowded with the usual suits. They took a booth in a darkened corner. Carson ordered himself a Guinness and Georgia opted for a pint of hard cider. They sat quietly for a few moments with their drinks. He didn't want to push her, but he needed the whole story. Brooks and Graham would be very interested in just how low Winchester had stooped today.

Georgia took a long sip of her drink and sighed heavily. "Well, the punch line is that he isn't going to back down on the land. He doesn't care if we're building a children's hospital or homes for one-legged orphan refugees. Well, actually that's not entirely true," she noted. "He said he might reconsider his position if I was willing to seriously consider his *generous* offer."

Carson's grip on his glass was so tight he worried he might crush the drink in his hand. "What was the offer?"

"First, he offered me a job as his director of public relations with a million-dollar signing bonus."

That didn't surprise him. Sutton was constantly cherry-picking employees from his competitors. They'd lost several high performers due to his below-the-belt tactics. But who offered a seven-figure bonus? "I never knew he was such a generous man," he said with a flat tone.

"I wouldn't call him that," she chuckled. "It came with some very important fine print. I was also to become his mistress. Then, and only then, would he consider backing down on the land project."

"Did he touch you inappropriately?" Carson hated to ask, but if Sutton crossed a line, Georgia could bring charges. She wasn't his employee yet, but at the very least they could file a civil suit and drag his name through the mud.

"Not really." Georgia rubbed her palms together thoughtfully. "He held my hand longer than I wanted him to, but it could've been a lot worse."

"Thank goodness," Carson said in a rush of breath he'd been holding. Just the thought of that old pervert laying a hand on Georgia made him want to punch his fist through the drywall. He felt bad enough about letting her go over there against his better judgment. If Sutton had gotten physically aggressive, Carson never would've forgiven himself. "I'm so sorry about all this. He's an even bigger pig than I expected. Where was Ron during all of this? I told you he had to escort you over there."

"He did. I just left him sitting in the waiting room as I told you I would."

"You didn't call for him when Sutton got inappropriate?"

"No. Like I said, he didn't really touch me. He just made me an offer I didn't accept," Georgia said with a guilty look. She held up her hand to silence him. "I know, I know. But I had it under control. My finger was on the trigger of my pepper spray the whole time. Sutton is bold, and certainly arrogant, but he's also smart. He's not going to have a woman run screaming from his office. It would hurt business."

That was probably true. The only thing Sutton Winchester liked more than women was money. He wasn't about to ruin his business and jeopardize his cash flow. It didn't make Carson feel any better. Georgia was confident in her ability to protect herself, but he had his doubts.

She was a petite woman. Curvy, but small. With

her platinum waves and knockout body, she drew men's eyes wherever she went. She had certainly drawn his gaze the first moment they met. A part of him hadn't wanted to hire her just so he could ask her out to dinner instead. In the end, his brain had overridden his erection. She was smart, experienced and the perfect candidate for the position.

"Georgia," he began, "I need to apologize to you."

"You just apologized. Really, Carson, it's not your fault. You warned me about what he was like. I just never dreamed he'd be that bold."

Carson shook his head. "I'm certainly sorry about what happened today, but that's not what I was apologizing for. I actually was talking about that kiss by the lake."

Georgia's soft, friendly expression hardened. He could tell she was uncomfortable with his bringing it up. "Carson, I—"

"No, let me say this," he interrupted. "In the moment, it felt like the right thing to do. But after what happened today, I realize just how inappropriate it was. If I don't recognize that, I'm just as bad as he is."

Georgia reached across the table and took Carson's hand. "You will never, ever be anything like that man. Don't even think that for a second."

Carson looked into her gray eyes, noting the touch of olive green that radiated from the center. It was an unusual color, one he'd never seen before. Her gaze seemed to penetrate him, as if she were seeing inside him in a way that made him uncomfortable. He looked down at their hands, which were still clasped atop the polished wood table.

It was only then that he allowed himself to notice how soft her skin felt against his. As he grasped her fingers, the blood started to hum in his veins. He remembered the sensation from the field, knew how long it would take him to recover from the reaction she stirred in him.

He didn't understand it. Georgia was beautiful, but Carson had touched his fair share of beautiful women. She was smart and funny, and he'd been around women like that, too. But never, not once since he broke the seal on his manhood in high school, had a woman affected him the way Georgia did. Lately all it took was the lingering scent of her perfume in the hallways at work, and he was consumed with thoughts of her.

Carson hated Sutton for putting the moves on Georgia, but he understood fully why he had done it. She had the power to enchant a man without even trying. A million dollars was chump change to Sutton, especially when it was a corporate write-off, but it was still a significant offer. If it came to it, what would Carson be willing to pay to keep her with him?

All that and more.

Looking up, he realized Georgia's expression had changed. She was no longer softly consoling him. Now her brow was lined with concern, and he realized it was because he was still holding her hand as though he might be repelled from the face of the earth if he didn't cling to her.

He immediately let her hand go and buried his own beneath the table. "I'm sorry. That probably just made it worse. I…I don't know why I have such a hard time maintaining a professional distance when I'm around you, Georgia. I've never had this problem before."

She nodded curtly and took another large drink, finishing off her glass without meeting his gaze. "I understand. We're both human, after all. We work together a lot, so the temptation is there. But we're strong, smart people. We can fight it."

Georgia said the words, but as he looked at her, he wasn't entirely sure she believed them. For the first time, the pieces started to click together in Carson's mind. She'd said "we," as in she was attracted to him, as well. That would certainly explain her flushed cheeks when he greeted her in the hallway and her more than enthusiastic response to his kiss. It was one thing for him to be attracted to her, but knowing the feeling was mutual would make this all ten times harder.

They needed to focus on work. That was what they were good at, what offered the best distraction. Going over their conversation about Sutton in his mind, he decided to talk strategy going forward.

"So what is our next step?" he asked. "We've got to secure that land no matter what Sutton wants."

A sly smile spread across Georgia's face. There was a twinkle of mischief in her gray eyes as she looked at him and said, "Next, we play dirty."

Smile. Look into the camera. Focus.

"I'd like to thank you all for coming today," Georgia began, ignoring the camera flashes and microphones in her face. Because she was PR director, press conferences fell into her job description, but she was always filled with nerves in front of the camera. Especially today. This was her moment to turn the tide with the land deal, and she couldn't screw it up.

"The Newport Corporation is a family company. It was founded by brothers Brooks, Graham and Carson Newport as a small real estate venture that turned into much more. CEO Carson Newport once told me that he knew they were a success when they were able to buy their mother, Cynthia Newport, a home and let her retire early.

"The love these three men had for their mother is why I've asked you to be here today. With her newfound free time, Cynthia discovered a purpose in working with sick children at the local hospital. She spent hours there reading stories, playing games and helping children forget—if for just a short time—about the pain and fear they lived with each day."

Georgia looked down at her notes and confirmed her next point. "The entire Newport Corporation was extremely saddened to hear about the sudden loss of Cynthia Newport two months ago. Without warning, she was stricken with a brain aneurysm, and there was nothing that could be done. She was only fifty-five years old.

"Cynthia's sons have decided that the best way to honor their mother's memory is to put their resources and expertise into the cause that was so dear to her heart. Ladies and gentleman," she said, reaching for the easel beside her, "I give you the plans for the Cynthia Newport Memorial Hospital for Children."

She removed a blank placard and revealed the artist's rendering of the hospital underneath. Georgia waited a moment for the cameras to stop flashing before she continued. "Newport Memorial will be the most sophisticated facility for children in the US. They will provide cutting-edge technology, the best treatment and the most skilled staff available."

Georgia spied Carson standing near the back of the crowd of reporters. Quite a few had showed up today for the press conference, huddling in a semicircle in the garden courtyard of the Newport building. Even then, he was easy to spot, especially with his brother, Brooks, beside him. The COO was almost always the tallest man in the room unless Graham was in the office. The two of them were like Norse gods in expensive suits.

Carson was like a demigod, half man, half immortal. Just real enough for her to feel like she could stand a chance with him, but enough of a fantasy to keep her pessimistic feet firmly planted on the ground.

Losing her place in the speech, she tore her gaze away and flicked over the neatly printed lines of the press statement. "After an exhaustive search, the Newport Corporation has identified an ideal spot for the hospital overlooking Lake Michigan. Unfortunately, we are not the only company with our eyes on the land. Recently, Elite Industries has announced, perhaps prematurely, their plans to build luxury condominiums along the water.

"It is our hope that with enough community support, we can make the Newport Memorial Hospital a reality, no matter how much money our competitors might try to throw around. The community needs this facility for our children far more than we need additional fancy housing for Chicago's wealthy."

She reached for the artist's rendering and set it aside to display a graphic of their social media campaign. "Show your support by posting on social media using the hashtag *#NewportMemorial4Kids* and letting the community know how you feel. Together, we can make this dream a reality. Now, I'll be taking any questions."

Georgia fielded about ten questions from the reporters about the project before ending the press conference. "Thank you," she said as she gathered up her note cards and slipped away from the podium. Moving through the crowd packing up their equipment, she found Carson and Brooks at the back where they'd been standing earlier. "How'd I do?" she asked.

"Amazing," Carson said with a pleased grin.

"There's no way Winchester's offer stands a chance with the seller after that." Brooks held up his cell phone. "Two of the stations aired this live, and there have already been over two hundred tweets under our hashtag. When this re-airs during the evening news, it will explode."

Georgia gave a heavy sigh of relief. She hoped this worked. If the owners were more interested in money, Winchester could still win them over.

After the press cleared out, they headed back upstairs to the executive floor. Brooks followed Carson into his office, where they poured a celebratory glass of scotch.

"Would you care for a drink, Georgia?" Brooks asked. "You certainly earned it."

"Actually, I think I'll pass," she said. The adrenaline that had gotten her though the press conference was fading, and she was ready to crash. "If you two don't mind, I think I'd like to catch an early train home and watch our segment on the news on the couch with some takeout."

She dismissed the flicker of disappointment on Carson's face. "Understandable," he said. "Keep the phone nearby, though. If the seller accepts our offer, you'll be the first person I call."

Georgia gave them a wave and slipped down the hallway to her office. She quickly gathered her things. If she could get to the "L" platform in the next ten minutes, she'd catch the express train.

She found herself at her building about a half hour later. Once she reached her apartment door, she gave a heavy sigh of relief. Georgia loved her loft. It was the first thing she'd bought when she secured her first real executive position with a major company. She could barely afford it at the time but she had been desperate to be able finally to have a home of her own.

She hadn't had the easiest time growing up. Her mother had been a teenage runaway when she was born. Georgia didn't remember much about those early years, but her caseworker, Sheila, had told her when she was older that her mother had developed a heroin addiction and was working as a prostitute for drugs. Georgia had been taken away and placed in foster care when she was only three.

From there, she'd become a Ping-Pong ball, bouncing from place to place. She never lived anywhere longer than a year, and none of those places ever felt like home. She tried not to let her mind dwell too much on her childhood in Detroit, but she'd let enough of the dirty homes, strict or even abusive foster parents and secondhand everything through to let her appreciate what she had now.

This loft, with its floor-to-ceiling windows and modern, industrial elements, was everything she'd ever wanted. The walls were painted in warm, inviting colors and the plush furniture was overflowing with pillows. The kitchen was state-of-the-art despite the fact that she never cooked. She could swim in her master bathtub and have a party in the shower. She had a service come in to clean once a week, so the place was always spotless.

It was wonderful. The perfect escape from the world. Even the longest, hardest day at the office couldn't keep the smile from her face when she walked in the door each evening.

Tonight she went through her nightly ritual. She set down her purse and disappeared into the bedroom to change. She reemerged ten minutes later with her blond hair in a knot on the top of her head, her face scrubbed free of makeup and her favorite pair of pajamas on. She poured herself a glass of pinot grigio and grabbed her favorite Chinese delivery menu before she collapsed on her suede sofa.

The delivery man arrived with her dinner with just minutes to spare before the evening newscast. The segment on the Newport Corporation was in the second news block when she was about halfway through her kung pao chicken. She didn't like watching herself on camera, but she forced herself to do it anyway. Her speech professor had made all the students do it. It was the only way to truly see the nervous ticks and language crutches she used when she spoke in public.

All in all, not bad. Her voice was sultry, like a phone sex operator, but there was nothing she could do about it. She'd tried a million times to alter it, but it sounded fake. On the upside, she used the word "uh" only twice and she didn't use "like" at all. Professor Kline would be very proud of her.

At the end of the segment, the news station flashed the campaign hashtag on the screen and encouraged viewers to use it to show their support. Georgia reached for her phone to check on the response. There were thousands of posts on Twitter with even more on other platforms. They were even trending.

Georgia chewed nervously at her thumbnail as she watched the posts scroll down the screen. This might actually work. She really, truly hoped so. The idea of Winchester taking that land and building condos on it made her stomach turn. She knew from experience that things weren't always fair or just in life, but she certainly hoped she was about to outsmart the system.

The rest of the newscast dragged on. She sat in front of the TV, idly chewing her dinner and not listening to anything. She was waiting for that phone to ring. It just had to ring.

She was on her second glass of wine when the news ended, and still no call. Georgia paced anxiously across the concrete floor, gazing out at her view of the city. The sun was just setting, making the Chicago skyline a stark silhouette against the golden glow of the sky. Lights were starting to turn on around town, slowly transforming the hard, industrial shapes of downtown into a sparkling constellation.

Georgia was so lost in her thoughts that when the phone rang, she jumped nearly six inches off the ground. Turning on her heel, she ran back to the kitchen and snatched her phone off the countertop. It was Carson.

She held her breath in anticipation as she picked up. "Yes?" she answered.

"Our offer has been accepted!" he announced triumphantly. "They said it was the highest and in the end, they decided to accept it and not start a bidding war because of the newscast. We got it, Georgia, and it's all because of your hard work."

"Thanks," she said, dismissing his compliment. "It's not hard to get behind a project like this when the lives of sick children are at stake. It made my work pretty easy, I have to say. I'm very happy our project can go forward."

"It will. Once the paperwork is signed, I want to have a grand groundbreaking ceremony. Your group will be heading up that effort. But first, we're going to kick off the project with a cocktail party on Friday night to celebrate. Rebecca is putting it together as we speak. Wear your dancing shoes."

Four

The sale was really happening. The lawyers were handling the details and it was off Georgia's plate. At least for now. Once the land was officially the property of the Newport Corporation, she would start the groundbreaking-ceremony preparation. After that, she had no doubt there would be charity fund-raiser events and a million other tasks on her plate to handle.

But tonight was for celebration, not work.

Carson's assistant had rented out a chic little bistro on the Magnificent Mile for the party. Wine was flowing like water, a jazz band was playing at a tasteful level in the corner and everyone was mingling and laughing. Every employee, from the janitor to the executives, had loved Cynthia. They knew how important this was to the brothers and were excited about this being the next new project on the agenda.

Folks had put on their fanciest cocktail attire for the night. At least, the women had. There was a rainbow of slinky and sparkly dresses in the room. Georgia herself had opted for a muted gold snakeskin cocktail dress by Tom Ford. It was a little showy, but with a high, scooped neck and long sleeves, it was also very modest, which she liked. The gold complemented her skin tone and brought out the darker tones of her platinum hair. The dress also didn't really need any jewelry to enhance it, so she'd been able to wear a simple pair of diamond stud earrings.

As usual, the men fell back on their arsenal of suits, although Georgia didn't mind a bit. She enjoyed the look of a man in a nice suit, especially the Newport brothers. Theirs were custom fitted to their broad shoulders and narrow hips. All three of them were milling around the room, drinks in hand. They were a ridiculously handsome trio, and every single woman in the room was eyeing the bachelors with interest. Except Georgia.

She turned away from them and glanced self-consciously around the room. She knew she should have been socializing, but she was happy to loiter at her cocktail table in the corner, watching the action. She loved working at the Newport Corporation. The people here were the family she'd never had.

But at the same time, she wasn't really great with this kind of social setting. Perhaps it was a handicap of her childhood. She'd moved too much to make friends and never had family she could count on. She watched the world go by from the fringe.

"Good evening, Georgia."

At the sound of a man's voice, Georgia turned to her left, startled. She was shocked to find Sutton Winchester standing so near her that they nearly brushed shoulders.

Biting down her irritation with him from earlier in the week, she smiled. "Good evening, Mr. Winchester." After all, she'd won the battle. She should have been happy to see him and gloat about her victory.

He held up a glass of white wine. "I got you a refill," he said.

Georgia looked down and noticed she had only half a sip left in her own glass. She set it on the table and accepted the fresh drink. "That was very thoughtful of you."

"I'm not a complete bastard," he said with a wry smile as he turned to look at the crowd she'd been eyeing a moment before.

"The jury is still out on that one."

Sutton chuckled heartily before it disintegrated into a string of harsh coughs. "Pardon me," he said, clearing his throat.

"So, what brings you to our little celebration tonight, Mr. Winchester? You don't have any pig's blood stashed in the rafters or anything, do you?"

"Not at all. I was actually invited," Sutton said with emphasis. "I'm sure the Newport boys want to rub their victory in my face. I'm happy to drink wine on their tab while they do it. Besides that, I wanted to talk to you."

"Me?" Georgia turned to him with her brow lifted in surprise.

"Yes. I saw your press conference the other day. I wanted to tell you what a good job you did with it. You worked the press and the social media outlets beautifully. The owner had no real choice but to sell to Newport after that. I underestimated your talent, Georgia. You're much more than just a pretty face. Knowing that makes me want you on my team even more. Come work for me. I'll bump that bonus up to 1.2 million dollars if you'll consider it."

Georgia couldn't believe the nerve of him to come into their celebration and proposition her again. "That's very generous of you, but I'm sorry, Mr. Winchester. The answer is still no." She glanced around the crowd, looking for an escape, but everyone seemed involved in other conversations.

He nodded, sipping his drink and pursing his lips in thought. "I understand you feel a sense of loyalty to the Newports, but this offer doesn't have to be a package deal. What about the *other* position we discussed?"

The other position? As his mistress? Every muscle
in Georgia's body tensed as she felt the older man
take in every inch of her. She hadn't been expecting
to see Sutton tonight. She was dressed quite differently than she had at his office. Her gold dress covered all the necessary skin, but it was clingy. And
short. And the back was completely bare to contrast
with the chaste front. She wished she was wearing a
caftan instead. Or that she could dump her wine on
him and tell the pervert to go to hell. But that was
unprofessional. She would hold it together and get
away from him as soon as she was able.

"I'm not interested in *any* of the offers," she said
as forcefully as she could. "It doesn't matter how
much money is involved."

Sutton narrowed his gaze at her. He looked a bit
befuddled, as though he didn't quite understand what
she was saying to him. He was a man used to getting
his way, and Georgia wasn't playing by his rules.
"May I ask why?"

Georgia searched her brain for a reason with
which he couldn't argue. He was a shrewd business-
man who could likely destroy any argument as surely
as an attorney during cross-examination. She didn't
want to leave any room for hope on his part.

"Georgia?" Sutton pressed.

"Fine," she said as the idea suddenly crystallized
in her mind. Good or bad, it was all she had. "I'm

not going to be your mistress because I already have a lover."

He looked shocked. Georgia wasn't certain if she should be insulted by his response. "Who?" he asked.

"Carson Newport." The words slipped from her lips before she could stop them, surprising even herself.

She wasn't the only one. Sutton's eyes were wide. He turned his head, and Georgia followed his gaze to where Carson was standing only a few feet away. He must have seen Sutton with her, because it looked as though he was on his way to rescue her from Winchester's clutches. Her words had stopped Carson cold. He was frozen in place, his drink clutched in his hand.

"Carson Newport is your lover?" Sutton asked with an incredulous tone.

Was it so unbelievable that a man like Carson would be interested in her? She didn't know what to say to his question. Georgia thought she might be caught in a lie. She hadn't expected Carson to overhear all of this. Now his reaction was key to selling her story. Before she could respond, Carson sidled up beside her and wrapped his arm around her waist.

"Surprised, Sutton?"

The old man turned to him and shrugged. "To be honest, I didn't think you had it in you, Carson."

Carson leaned in to nuzzle Georgia's ear and plant a searing kiss on the sensitive skin on her neck. "Go with it," he whispered softly.

She tried to do as he said and not tense in his arms, even as a thrill of arousal ran through her body. Leaning into his touch, she let her eyes flutter closed for a moment. If she was being honest with herself, it wasn't hard to feign interest in him. Such a simple touch had lit up her nerves like Christmas lights.

She opened her eyes in time to see Carson turn back to Sutton with a grin. "You're not having the best week, are you? You were after waterfront property and a woman, and I bested you on both. You must be losing your touch, old man."

With a clenched jaw, Sutton looked over both of them and slammed back the last of his drink. "I'm not the kind of man who gives up that easily, Carson. Enjoy her while you can," he suggested before turning on his heel and stomping through the crowd to the exit.

Once he was gone, Georgia took a step away from Carson and covered her mouth with her hand to smother her embarrassment. "Oh, Carson," she said. "I am so sorry. He put me on the spot and it just came out."

Carson put a reassuring hand on her shoulder and shook his head. "Not to worry. It did the trick, for now, at least. I wouldn't count on him letting it go entirely. Like he said, he's not that kind of man. Then again, who would want to compete with me for a woman's affections?"

At that, Georgia giggled, and the tension of the

moment slipped away. Thank goodness he hadn't read more into her naming him as her lover. "Hopefully no one was listening in on the conversation. I'd hate for rumors to start about us."

"Oh, I'd say half the room heard you blurt out my name, but don't worry about the rumors. Your boss knows it isn't true, and he's the only one who can fire you."

"I'm relieved to hear that. The last thing I want to do is put my position at the Newport Corporation in jeopardy."

"Well, if nothing else, I hear Sutton has a position open," he said with laughter lighting his eyes. "Come on," Carson said, slipping a comforting arm around her shoulder to guide her into the crowd. "No more hiding in the corner. This is your party, too. Let's celebrate."

Carson never went into the office on a Saturday if he could avoid it. He always tried to make the most of his time away from work so he could have a life. Or at least, so he'd have the time to have a life when he actually decided to get around to it.

The Newport brothers passed that same work-life balance philosophy on to their employees. That was why Carson was so surprised to see a light on when he walked down the hallway. It was Georgia's office.

Curious, he paused in the doorway, hoping not to scare her. She was working intently at her computer, probably not expecting anyone to appear suddenly. He took the quiet moment to admire her without her knowing it. There was just something so appealing about Georgia. Of course, she was the blonde bombshell that most men desired, but even the little things drew him to her. At the moment, he found the crease between her eyebrows as she concentrated on her work appealing.

Today her hair was in a casual ponytail, something she would never wear to the office on an average workday. She was wearing a tight-fitting T-shirt and jeans. Carson realized in that moment that he'd never seen Georgia look like this before. She was always so professional and put together, even on a casual Friday. He appreciated that about her, but she looked so much younger and more easygoing today.

"You know, it's rude to stare."

Busted. Carson grinned wide and met Georgia's amused gaze. "I wasn't expecting to see anyone here today. Nor did I think I'd find you in jeans."

Georgia looked down self-consciously at herself. "Is that okay? I didn't think anyone would see me. I'm usually here alone on the weekends."

"It's absolutely fine," he said, although he was concerned by the rest of her response. "Are you here most weekends?"

"Yes. I like the quiet of the office. It lets me catch up on things and focus without calls or people com-

ing by. I know the company is big on spending time
with family, but I don't have a family."

Carson tried not to frown. He didn't know much
about Georgia. She was all work during business
hours, so they hadn't spent much time socializing.
Her office was tidy and well decorated, but there
weren't any photos of family or friends on her desk
or bookshelves. Now he knew why.

"What about you?" she asked. "Why are you in
today? I thought after all that champagne last night
that most people would be laid out until noon at
least."

He had woken with a slight headache, but nothing he couldn't handle. As for why he was here, that
was a good question. He'd gotten into his car, fully
intending to drive to his mother's home and make
good on his promise to clean out the house. The next
thing he knew, he was at work. "I thought I'd come
in and check on some things."

Georgia wrinkled her nose. "You're avoiding
something," she said without a touch of doubt in
her voice.

He sighed and slumped against her door frame.
Was he that transparent? "I guess I am."

"Anything I can help you with?"

Whereas he hadn't been looking to drag anyone
into the slog of work, he realized that he didn't dread
the task so much when he envisioned Georgia there

with him. "No, no. You've probably got better things to do," he argued.

"No, tell me," Georgia insisted.

"I'm supposed to be cleaning out my mother's house. I told Brooks and Graham that I'd go through everything and start getting it ready to sell. That's where I intended to go today, but I ended up here instead. I don't know why."

"I can imagine that would be difficult," she said. "Would you like me to go with you? I'd be happy to lend a hand. At the very least, I can offer moral support."

It sounded great, but he still felt anxious about it. "Are you sure? Her house is about a half hour from here, up in Kenilworth."

Georgia closed her laptop and stood up. She picked up her massive black purse and slung it over her arm. "I'm sure. Let's go."

He wasn't going to argue with her. Without even making it as far as his own office, they turned around and headed back to the elevator.

They were on the expressway north before they spoke again. "So tell me," Georgia began, "what's going on here? I mean, if you don't mind. I get the feeling this is about more than just sorting through your mother's things."

Carson gripped the leather-wrapped steering wheel and focused his gaze intently on the traffic ahead of him. "Do you really want to know my tragic life story?"

Georgia snorted delicately. "I think I can trump you on tragic life stories."

"Tell me about you, then." Carson was far more interested in Georgia's life than he was in rehashing his own.

She shook her head adamantly. "Nope. I asked you first. And besides, this trip is about you. I need to know if I'm treading into a mine field here."

His brothers wanted him to dig up the truth about their father. If she was going to be there helping him, she needed to know. "Okay," he relented. "My mother is the only real family we ever had. Our aunt Gerty died a long time ago, and she wasn't really related to us. Losing Mom, we lost any connection we have to our roots. It's been a difficult realization for us all."

"I understand what that can be like," Georgia said without elaborating. "Did your mother ever speak about her family or your father to you?"

"Rarely, and when we pushed her, nothing she said was good. She insisted that our father was abusive and she ran away from him in the middle of the night when we were still babies. She never would tell us where we lived before, his name or anything about the past. She made it very clear that she didn't want us to find him when we were older."

"That must be frustrating for you all," Georgia

noted. "Wanting to belong, yet having that fear that the truth would be worse than being alone."

"Exactly," Carson said with surprise in his voice. He didn't expect her to be able to understand it all so easily. "Brooks and Graham want me to look for clues in the house. They seem convinced that the answers are hidden away somewhere. I'm not so sure, but I told them I would look. It's our last chance at the truth. The rest died with Mom."

That was probably the hardest part. Carson had gotten the feeling that maybe one day their mother might tell them the rest of the story. They weren't children anymore. She had nothing to fear from her past because the boys could protect her, no matter what. Cynthia probably thought she had time to share the whole tale about where they came from, and then it was stolen away in an instant.

"I'll help you find out the truth," Georgia said.

As Carson exited the expressway and headed toward the house in Kenilworth, he found himself nearly overwhelmed with gratitude that she was here with him. That she understood. "Thank you" was all he could verbalize.

"I don't know my real family, either," she offered. "I grew up in the Detroit foster care system because my mother was a teenage runaway. She got into drugs and a lot of other nasty things and they took me away. I have no idea who my father is or anything about my family. My father's name was left off the birth certificate. I don't even know for certain that my last name is really Adams. She could've just picked that name out of the sky. Not having that link to your past and where you come from can make you feel like discarded paper drifting on the wind."

Carson was surprised by her confession, but it made a lot of the pieces of the Georgia puzzle fall into place. Maybe that's why he was so drawn to her. They were both lost, anchorless. "Have you kept contact with your mother at all over the years?"

"No," she said, shaking her head and looking down into her hands folded in her lap. "I haven't seen her since I was three and social services came for me. I wouldn't really even know what she looked like if my caseworker, Sheila, hadn't given me an old photo of her. I keep it in my purse." Georgia reached for her bag and pulled out the photo.

Carson turned in to his mother's driveway just as she handed over the picture. He put the car in Park and studied the worn photograph. The blonde girl in the picture was holding a towheaded toddler. She looked very young, not more than fifteen or sixteen. The late '80s influences were evident in her big hair and heavy makeup, which didn't hide the dark circles under her eyes or the hollowed-out cheeks. There were purple track marks on the girl's arm.

"I think she looked a lot like me, but thinner. Harder. There wasn't much life in her eyes by that point. Aside from that, I don't have any memories of her that really stayed with me. I just remember the homes."

In that moment, Carson was extremely thankful to his mother for everything she'd done for him and his brothers. They hadn't had much, but she'd done all she could to keep them safe and healthy. Georgia hadn't been so lucky. He handed the photo back to her. "Did you move around a lot?"

Georgia chuckled bitterly as she put the picture away. "You could say that. It was a blessing and a curse. If the family was horrible, I had the solace of knowing I wouldn't be there long. If they were amazing and kind, I would cry every night knowing that eventually I would have to leave. The only constant in my life was Sheila. In a way, she became my family. She's the one that helped me get into college by helping me write a million scholarship essays. She insisted that I make something of myself."

"That was my aunt Gerty for us. She took us in after her husband died and made us her family. When she passed away, she left enough money for my brothers and me to go to college and start our business. Our mother insisted that we become the best version of ourselves we could possibly be. Without that kick start, I'm not sure what would've become of us. Everything we are is because of my mother and Gerty."

Georgia reached out in that moment and took his hand. Her touch was warm and enveloping, like a comforting blanket. They sat for a moment in the driveway, silently acknowledging all that they'd shared.

His mother's home stood like a monolith in front of them. Inside were all the memories, secrets and emotions of her life. Going inside felt like disturbing her grave somehow.

"Are you ready?" Georgia prompted him after a few minutes.

"No, but let's go inside anyway."

They climbed from his Range Rover and walked together toward the front door. Carson unlocked it and they stepped into the tile foyer. The house had always seemed so warm and welcoming before, but now it was cold and silent like a tomb. His mother had given it life.

"Where should we start?"

Carson looked around and pointed toward the staircase. "Let's focus on her bedroom. If she was keeping any kind of secrets, I think that's where they'd be."

"Okay." Georgia started for the stairs, but paused and turned back when Carson didn't follow her. Her gray eyes questioned him.

Thank goodness she was here. He wouldn't even have made it this far without her prompting. It was better this way. Get it done, get it over with. If Carson didn't find anything about their family history, so be it. At least he and his brothers could move on with their lives. "I'm coming."

Georgia reached out her hand to him until he took it. "My past may be buried forever, but we're going to find your family, Carson. I can feel it."

Five

Carson was getting discouraged. They'd gone through almost everything in his mother's bedroom. Drawer by drawer, box by box, they'd sorted through for any personal effects and then bagged the remaining items up. Some clothes and accessories were for donation, some things were for the dump, and others, like her jewelry, were to be split up among the brothers.

Hours had gone by without a single discovery of interest. No skeletons under the bed, no dark secrets hidden away in the underwear drawer. They'd checked the pocket of every coat and the contents of each old purse. Nothing but used tubes of lipstick and some faded receipts. All that was left was a collection of shoe boxes on the very top shelf of the closet.

Carson eyed the boxes with dismay. They were likely to find nothing but shoes in them. Most of the boxes seemed like fairly new acquisitions from her life after he and his brothers had made their fortune—Stuart Weitzman, Jimmy Choo, Christian Louboutin… But one box caught his eye. On the very top of the stack, in the far back corner, was a ratty old box with a faded and curling Hush Puppies label on it. There was no doubt that box had been around in his mother's closet for a very long time. Maybe even thirty years or so…

"There's a shoe box in the very back corner that looks promising," Carson said. Looking around, he was annoyed to find that it was out of his reach even with his height and long arms. "How can my mother not own a stepladder or something? I guess I'll run downstairs and get a chair."

"No," Georgia insisted. "I'm sure I can reach it. I just need you to give me a boost."

Carson looked at her with concern. "A boost?"

"Yes, just make a step for me to put my foot in your hands and boost me up. I'll be able to reach it."

It would be just as easy to go get a chair, but he wasn't going to argue with her. He wanted into that box as soon as possible. Crouching over, Carson laced his fingers together and made a steady perch for Georgia's shoe.

"One, two, three," she counted, hoisting herself up.

Carson held her up and patiently waited for news. "Can you reach it?"

"It's just beyond me. Hold on. Wait… I've… almost…got it!" A moment later, it came tumbling off the top shelf along with several others. Georgia lost her balance and dropped from his hands, colliding with his chest.

"Whoa there," he said, catching her before she could bounce off him and hit the floor. He'd instinctively wrapped his arms around her, holding her body tight against his own. The contact sent a surge of need through his veins, making him hyperaware of her breasts molded to his chest. Every muscle in his body tightened, his pulse quickening in his throat as he held her. "Are you okay?" he asked as he swallowed hard.

She looked up at him with momentarily dazed eyes. "Yeah… I mean *yes*. I wasn't expecting it to all rain down at once." She pressed gently but insistently against his chest. Carson relinquished his hold and she took a step back. He breathed in deeply to cool his arousal and tried to focus on their discovery instead.

Georgia looked down at the floor of the closet and the mess they'd made. There were several pairs of shoes scattered around the floor. The shoe box they'd sought out, the oldest one in the bunch with the peeling Hush Puppies label, had come open, too. As expected, there was not a thirty-year-old pair of shoes in it. Instead the paper contents had scattered everywhere, making the closet look as if a blizzard had struck.

They both crouched down and started sorting through the mess. Carson found a few pictures bundled together with a piece of twine. He untied them and sifted through the images. A couple were of him and his brothers when they were small. Things like Christmas morning and school pageants. There was one of his mother when she was very young, maybe even a teenager. After that were a few with his mother and some other people he didn't recognize. He flipped the pictures over, but there was no writing on the back, no clue as to whether the other people were family or friends.

Setting them aside, he picked up some old newspaper clippings. Most of the pieces were about a missing girl named Amy Jo Turner. He scanned one of the articles looking for clues about his mother, but all it talked about was the circumstances surrounding the teenager's disappearance and how the authorities presumed the worst. Her boat had been found drifting empty in a lake. A single shoe and the sweater she was last seen in had washed up a mile away about a week later.

The header was for a paper in Houston, Texas, and the dates were all in the early '80s before Brooks and Graham were born. Their mother had never mentioned Houston, much less that she might have lived there at some point. Who was Amy Jo Turner? What did any of this have to do with his mother? It was important enough for her to keep the clippings for thirty years, but he didn't understand why.

"Carson," Georgia said, drawing his eye from the photos. "Look at this."

He took a discolored envelope from her hand and unfolded the letter inside it. It was a handwritten letter addressed to his mother. Impatient, he skimmed through the words to the bottom where it was signed "Yours always, S." Returning to the top, he read through it again, looking for clues to the identity of the writer that he might have missed the first time.

Dearest Cynthia,
You don't know how hard it's been to be away from you. I know that I've put myself in this position, and I can't apologize enough. I seem to destroy everything that I love. You and the boys are probably better off without me. I hope that one day you can forgive me for what I've done to you. Know that no matter how much time has passed, my feelings for you will never fade. You have been, and always will be, the one true love of my life.
Yours always, S

That was totally and completely useless. All Carson got from it was an initial. He flipped over the envelope to look at the postmark. The date sent a sudden surge of adrenaline through him. It was a Chicago postmark dated seven months before he was born. *That* meant something. Could this lover, this "S," actually be his father? Why couldn't the man have written his name and made it easier on them all?

"What do you think?" Georgia asked tentatively after a few minutes.

Turning the letter over in his hand, Carson ran his gaze over the words one last time. "I think the person who wrote this letter is my father. It's the biggest lead I've ever had and yet somehow, I don't feel like I'm any closer to finding out his identity than I was before. What good is one initial?"

"It's more than you had before," she said in an upbeat tone.

Carson wasn't feeling quite as optimistic. "Anything else interesting?" he asked.

Georgia shuffled through some more envelopes that were bound together with a rubber band. "These are old pay stubs. She's kept them going back for years and years. Other than that, not much, sorry."

Carson nodded and started putting everything back into the shoe box. "That's okay. We found something. That should make my brothers happy. I'll hand this over to them and let them analyze to their hearts' content. Let's pack up the last of these shoes and call it a day."

They slowly gathered up all the bags and boxes and hauled them downstairs to the foyer. When he looked down at his watch, Carson realized he'd kept Georgia here far longer than he'd expected to. "Wow, it's late. I'm sorry about that. I hijacked your whole Saturday."

Georgia set down a bag of clothes and shrugged. "I would've spent it working anyway. I told you I'd help. I didn't put a time limit on it."

"Well, thank you. I got through that faster with you here. I might have given up long before I found that box. There's still more to go through, but I think what I was looking for is right here," he said, holding the old shoe box. "I'd like to make it up to you. May I buy you dinner?"

Georgia studied his face for a moment, her pert nose wrinkling as she thought it over. Finally she said, "How do you feel about Chinese takeout?"

"Can you pass me the carton of fried rice?"

Georgia accepted the container and used some chopsticks to shovel a pile out onto her plate beside her sesame chicken and spring roll. The Chinese place a block from her loft was the best in town. She ate there at least three times a week. Carson hadn't seemed too convinced about her dinner suggestion at first. He must have wanted to take her someplace nice with linen napkins or something, but she'd insisted.

They drove back downtown to her place, then walked up the street together to procure a big paper bag full of yum and grab a six-pack of hard cider from the corner store. That was her idea, too. Lobster and expensive wine were nice, but honestly, nothing topped a couple of cartons of Jade Palace delicacies eaten around the coffee table.

"Wow," Carson said after taking a bite of beef and broccoli. "This is really good."

"I told you. It's all amazing. And really, you have to eat it while you sit on the floor. It adds to the experience."

Carson chuckled at her and returned to his food. She'd expected him to turn his nose up at eating on the floor around her coffee table, but he'd gone with it. She had a dining room table, but she almost never ate there. It was the place where she worked on her laptop, not ate.

"I lived with a family for a while that ate every meal around the coffee table," Georgia explained. "They didn't watch television or anything. It was just where they liked to be together. There were about six of us who would crowd around it and eat every night, talking and laughing. I really enjoyed that."

"Those moments are the best ones," Carson agreed. "There are some days when I'd give up every penny I've ever earned to be a kid again, watching old movies and eating popcorn with Aunt Gerty and Mom. My brothers and I get together and do it every few weeks, but it's not the same."

Georgia watched her boss's face softly crumble

into muted sadness as he stared down at his plate, shoveled some chicken into his mouth and chewed absentmindedly. She knew what it was like to miss people that you could never have back in your life. She'd always consoled herself with the idea that there was something better in her future. "You'll make new moments," she reassured him. "And one day when you have a family of your own, your children will treasure the little things you share with them just the same."

"That feels like it won't happen for decades. Honestly, just the idea of a family of my own seems impossible. I work so much. And even if I found the perfect woman, I'd feel like a fraud somehow. How can I be a father when I don't know what it's like to have one?"

"You'll figure it out. Just start by being there and you'll already have both our fathers beat. You're a good guy, Carson. I have no doubt that it will come naturally to you."

"What about you? You're not going to have a family of your own while you spend all your free time at work."

Georgia knew that. A part of her counted on it. What good was starting a relationship when it was just going to end? People always left her—life had proven that much—so she kept her relationships casual and avoided more disappointment. "Right now, the Newport Corporation and its employees are my family. The only family I've ever had. For now, that's enough for me."

"So you're not dating anyone?" Carson asked.

Georgia's gaze met his with curiosity. Was he really fishing for information or just being polite? "Haven't you heard? Carson Newport is my lover." She punctuated the sentence by popping the last bite of food into her mouth and putting her chopsticks across the plate in disgust. She could really put her foot in her mouth sometimes.

Carson chuckled and set aside his own utensils. Leaning onto his hand, he looked at her over the coffee table and said, "Can I ask you something?"

"Why not?" she said. They'd already covered their painful childhoods. What could be worse than that?

"Why did you tell Sutton I was your lover last night?"

That. That could be worse. "I, uh…" Georgia started, but couldn't think of anything else to say. "It just popped into my head," she said as she got up and carried a few dishes into the kitchen.

Carson didn't let her escape. He followed her with the last of their dinner and set it on the counter beside her. "That's it?" he asked as he leaned his hip against the counter. He was so near to her that her senses were flooded with the scent of his cologne and the heat of his body.

With a sigh, Georgia turned to face him. This wasn't junior high; she needed to be a grown-up

about this. The movement put her so close to him
that they almost touched, but she felt childish taking a step back. "It was just wishful thinking," she
said, letting her gaze fall to the collar of his shirt.

Carson's hand came to rest at her waist. "Georgia?" he asked softly.

She almost couldn't answer with him touching
her. The hem of her T-shirt just barely brushed the
waistband of her jeans, and his fingers had come to
rest in part on her bare skin. It was a simple touch,
and yet it made her heart stutter in her chest and her
breath catch in her throat. "Yes?"

He hooked his finger under her chin and tilted
her head up until she had no choice but to look at
him. She felt her cheeks flush with embarrassment
and a touch of excitement as her gaze met his. His
sea-green eyes searched her face as his lips tipped
upward in a smile of encouragement. "I was hoping
you'd say that."

Georgia almost couldn't hear him for the blood
rushing in her ears. Had that kiss the other day been
more than just excitement and champagne? "Why?"

Carson slid his hand around to her lower back,
pulling her body flush against his own. "Because
I lie in bed at night and think about that kiss we
shared. I've fantasized about holding you in my arms
again. I know that I shouldn't because you work for
me, but I can't help it. And now that you've announced to half the company that we're lovers and

the world didn't end… I don't have any reason to
hold back any longer."

The longer he spoke, the more she fell under his
spell. He was right. Their work relationship could
survive this if they handled it like adults. They were
attracted to each other. A little indulgence couldn't
hurt. It wouldn't turn into anything serious and im-
pact their business dealings. No one else seemed to
care except Sutton.

"Then don't," she said, boldly meeting his gaze.

He took her at her word. Carson's lips met hers
without hesitation. His kiss was powerful yet not
overwhelming. Georgia stood on tiptoe to wrap her
arms around his neck and draw herself closer to him.
When his tongue sought her out, she opened to him
and melted into his touch.

She had thought the kiss at the hospital property
was amazing, but that was nothing, nothing like this.
This kiss was like a lightning bolt to her core. As his
hands rubbed her back and his fingers pressed into
her flesh, all she could think about was how badly
she needed Carson.

"I want you," she whispered against his lips.

Carson broke away from her mouth and trailed
kisses along her jawline to the sensitive hollow of
her neck. "You're going to have me," he said in a low
growl at her ear.

His mouth returned to hers, hungrier than before.
This was no longer just a simple kiss. It was officially

foreplay. Without breaking the kiss, he walked them backward through the kitchen until her legs met with the dining room table. Georgia eased up onto it until she was sitting on it with Carson nestled snugly between her denim-clad thighs. She could feel his desire pressing against her, sending a shiver of need down her spine.

Carson slipped his hand beneath her shirt to stroke the smooth skin of her back and press her even closer to him. He gripped the hem and in one fluid move pulled her T-shirt up and over her head, throwing it to the floor. He took in the overflowing cups of her bra before he reached over his shoulder to tug his own shirt off.

His mouth moved quickly to her collarbone, traveling lower to taste her breasts. Georgia unfastened her bra and slipped it off her arms. She didn't want anything else between them. This was the skin-on-skin contact she'd craved, and she wanted it now.

Carson groaned at the sight of her before he covered both her breasts with his hands. She felt her nipples tighten as his palms grazed over them. He moved his lips and tongue over her skin, tasting every inch of her exposed flesh before he drew one tight bud into his mouth.

"Carson!" she cried out as the sharp stab of pleasure shot straight to her inner core. She arched her back, pressing herself closer to him and to the touch she desperately craved.

"I can't believe this is really happening," she gasped as she looked up at the ceiling.

He planted a kiss on her sternum. "Believe it, beautiful."

Georgia closed her eyes and gave in to the sensations he was eliciting from her body. Just when she thought she couldn't take any more of his pleasurable torture, she felt his hand slide down her stomach to her jeans. She lifted her hips as he slid them and her panties down her legs.

As he stood, his eyes devoured her naked body. Reaching into his pants pocket, he pulled out a condom and set it on the table beside her. He kissed her again and let his hand wander over her bare thigh as he did. Carson dipped his fingers between her legs, brushing over her sensitive skin and sending a shiver through her whole body.

He did it again, harder, and this time Georgia cried aloud when he made contact. "Do you like that?" he asked.

"Oh yeah," she said.

Encouraged by her response, he stroked again and again until she was panting and squirming at the edge of the table. He built up the release inside her so quickly, she could hardly believe it until it was almost too late.

"Stop," she gasped, gripping his wrist with her hand. "Not yet. I want you inside me."

"Very well," Carson agreed. His gaze never left

hers as he unfastened his pants and sheathed himself quickly. He settled back between her legs, and Georgia felt him press against her.

"Yesss," she hissed as he slowly sank into her.

Carson hooked his hands around the backs of her knees and tugged her to the very edge of the table. If he let go, she'd fall, so she wrapped her legs around his rib cage and drew him in deeper. Judging by his sharp intake of breath, he wasn't going anywhere.

He gripped her hips, holding her steady as he started to move in her. Every stroke set off fire bursts beneath her eyelids as they fluttered closed. Georgia arched her back and braced her hands on the table as their movements became more desperate.

How had she even gotten here? This morning, she'd gone into work with few expectations for the day. By nightfall, she was fulfilling her biggest fantasy with Carson and on the verge of an amazing orgasm. She could feel it building inside her. He coaxed the response from her body so easily, as though they were longtime lovers.

"So close," she said between ragged breaths.

Carson seemed to know just what to do to push her over the edge. Rolling his hips forward, he thrust harder, striking her sensitive core with each advance. In seconds, Georgia was tensing up in anticipation of her undoing.

Then it hit. It radiated through her body like a nuclear blast. She clung to Carson's shoulders as the shockwaves of pleasure made every muscle tremble and quiver. They rode though it together. With her final gasp, her head dropped back and her body went limp in his arms.

"Georgia," he groaned, thrusting hard into her. He surged forward and gasped against the curve of her throat as he poured into her.

Georgia cradled him against her bare chest as he recovered. Thoughts swirled through her mind as the sexual haze faded away and she realized she'd just had sex with her boss on the dining room table.

Before she could say anything, Carson straightened up and wrapped his arms around her waist. He lifted her from the table and carried her through the living room. "Bedroom?" he asked.

"Upstairs," she said.

"Of course it is."

With a smile, he carried her upstairs to the master suite that overlooked the downstairs. He placed her gently on the bed and moved quickly to strip off his remaining clothes before crawling onto the mattress beside her. He tugged her back against him and wrapped his arms around her waist.

Georgia was surprised to find him ready for her so quickly. "Again?" she asked.

"Oh yes. And this time, it will be in a proper bed."

"At least I can say I used the dining room table this year," she said with a wicked grin.

Six

"You won't believe what I've dug up!"

Brooks and Carson were talking business in Carson's office when Graham charged in with his bold declaration. Carson had been waiting for this moment since he turned over the shoe box to his older brothers. It had been nearly a week since the discovery and his encounter with Georgia.

After giving Graham the box of paperwork, Carson had returned his focus to Georgia. Work had sucked up the majority of their time, as usual, but he was looking forward to the weekend and having another chance to meet up with her outside the office. At work, she was too tense. Despite the fact that he didn't care if anyone knew they were seeing one another, she still wasn't comfortable with it.

The contents of the shoe box had slipped his mind as the final paperwork on the hospital property went through and the finishing touches were put on the plans. Then Graham burst through his office door and it all came back to him.

Graham flopped into a chair at the table where Brooks and Carson were sitting. There was a light of excitement in his blue eyes, like he'd get when he had a breakthrough in a legal case. They'd given him the box because sorting through paperwork and finding clues was his specialty as a lawyer. Carson would've fallen asleep before he found anything important.

"Well?" Brooks prompted after several moments of silence.

"Well," Graham began, "as I went through everything, I was surprised to find a few months' worth of pay stubs from Elite Industries. Apparently Mom went to work there right before Brooks and I were born and stayed until seven months before she had you, Carson."

Carson frowned. She'd never mentioned that, not once in all those years. Not even when they complained about their competitor around the dinner table. "I thought she worked as a waitress at the café with Gerty."

"She did until she was in the third trimester of her pregnancy with Brooks and me. She went back to the diner again after her time with Elite. It looks as though she was laid off from her job after six months, although I don't know why. The paperwork I found showed she was given a very generous severance package and a glowing letter of reference from her boss when she left. Guess who she worked for at Elite? Starts with an S…"

Carson's stomach started to ache. He didn't really want to know where this was headed.

"Sutton Winchester?" Brooks guessed with as much dread in his voice as Carson was feeling.

"Yep," Graham confirmed, nearly boiling over with excitement. "She was his executive assistant."

Carson pushed up from his chair and shook his head. "I need a drink. Anyone else?"

"I think we all could use one," Brooks said.

Carson busied himself pouring them each a finger of scotch over ice. He carried the three short tumblers to the conference table and flopped back down into his chair with a sigh of disgust. Without waiting on his brothers, he took a large sip of the scotch, savoring the burn as it rushed down his throat into his empty stomach.

"So Mom was his executive assistant? That's a big leap from a coffee shop waitress," Brooks noted with a frown as he picked up his own glass.

It was. How could she have possibly qualified for a job like that? Knowing what Carson knew about Sutton, the answer wasn't one he wanted to consider.

Would his mother really have accepted that sleaze's secretarial position when it came with sexual duties? Especially when she was seven months pregnant with twins? Or was she already his lover long before she went to work for him?

"Carson?" Graham said with concern in his voice. "Are you okay? You look a little pale."

He understood why. He could feel the blood draining from his face as the reality of their past solidified in his mind. He hadn't had enough scotch to handle this. No wonder their mother didn't want them to know the truth. No wonder she said their father was a horrible person. He was. Still, he had trouble believing it could be true. It just couldn't be. And yet... he knew the truth almost instinctively.

"He's our father," Carson blurted out.

Brooks narrowed his gaze suspiciously at Carson. "How can you be so sure?"

"The letter I showed you guys the other day from the box. It talks about hurting her, missing her terribly and how sorry he was about everything that happened. How she and the boys would be better off without him. It's signed 'S.'"

"That's still a bit of a stretch," Brooks argued. "There are a lot of people with a first name starting with *S* in the world."

"Yes, but we're talking about Sutton Winchester here. I don't know if I told both of you, but when he demanded that Georgia meet with him, he offered her quite a sweet deal to come work for Elite Industries. The job came with a million-dollar signing bonus and the role of his mistress."

Graham's mouth dropped open, his glass of scotch hanging in his hand midair. "Are you serious? That old dog!"

Carson nodded gravely. "If that's how Sutton recruits employees *and* lovers, it all makes sense. Say he met Mom at the diner and they started an affair. When she ends up pregnant, he offers her the job as his assistant so she would have medical benefits and maternity leave. Being on her feet all day carrying twins had to be rough on her. I can see why she would accept the offer, especially if she was put on bed rest or something until you two were born."

Brooks looked at him thoughtfully. "If he went to all that trouble when she was pregnant the first time, why would he fire her when she was pregnant with you? It seems inconsistent."

Carson shook his head. "I don't know why. But I think it all goes back to the letter I found in the shoe box. It sounds to me like it might not have been Sutton's decision to let her go."

"Well," Graham said, "he was married at the time. Do you think his wife found out about his family on the side and made him put an end to all of it?"

Brooks chuckled. "Have you *met* Celeste Van Houten? She's one icy-cold woman. I wouldn't put it past her."

"We need proof," Graham argued and ran his fingers through his blond hair. "If we want to know the truth, once and for all, we'll need a paternity test. I doubt the old man will just go along with it to be nice, especially when it would mean we'd be eligible for a chunk of that multimillion-dollar estate of his when he dies. There's no way I can compel a paternity test just on the basis of our mother having been his employee at the time of Carson's conception. We need something that shows they actually had an affair."

"Who would know aside from the two of them?" Brooks asked.

"That's a tough one. Sutton wasn't likely to broadcast what he was doing, even though it looks obvious to us."

"Someone would have to know," Carson insisted. "Maybe someone who worked for Sutton at the time at his office or his house."

"That's someplace we can start," Graham agreed. "I'll do some more digging and see what I can find. Maybe we'll luck out and find someone who still remembers that far back. It's been thirty years."

Carson knew Graham was trying to be upbeat, but he could hear the discouragement in his voice. The odds of finding someone who knew about their mother's relationship were pretty low. Most of Sutton's employees were probably paid handsomely to keep their mouths shut. But if anyone could track them down, Graham could.

"It's more than we knew a week ago," Brooks said.

"That's true," Carson agreed. "I just wonder what the point of it would be."

"What do you mean?" Graham asked.

"Well, we take the paternity test and we find out he's our father. Then what? I don't see this ending well."

"It won't, at least not for Sutton," Brooks said. "We're going to make him pay for what he did to our mother and to us."

"How?" Carson asked. "The man has no conscience."

"That's true," Brooks agreed. "But he does have a multimillion-dollar estate and we would be rightful heirs to it as well as his three legitimate daughters with Celeste. We go in and demand our share as his penance. I don't care if we blow it all in a year, as long as we pry it from his cold, dead hands."

"Wouldn't most of the estate go to his wife?"

Graham shook his head. "Celeste is his ex-wife now and has been for a couple years. Her lawyers have already seized her share. The rest of his estate most likely goes to his daughters. No matter what, Sutton can change the will to include us if he wants to. We just have to give him a little encouragement."

Carson tried not to frown. It all made sense. Sutton deserved it. He just didn't like it. "Okay," he said. "We find a way to push for a test, then go after the estate. There's just one downside to all of this."

"What's that?"

"If we're right, it means that Sutton Winchester is our father. Mom warned us up one side and down the other to stay away from our father. She said he was dangerous and we were far better off without him in our lives. I always thought that maybe she had exaggerated and that when we met him, we'd find he was a better man that we expected. But if it *is* Sutton… I worry that our worst fears about our father are about to come true."

"Georgia?"

Georgia looked up from her barely touched dinner and found Carson looking at her with concern. She was lost in her thoughts and he'd caught her not listening.

After fantasizing about time alone with Carson for so long, she was letting it slip through her fingers. Tonight he'd insisted on taking her out to dinner someplace nice. He was wearing her favorite navy pinstripe suit. For some reason, that color against his tan skin made his green eyes pop. He was looking so handsome and yet she could barely focus on a word he said.

"Yes?"

"Are you okay? You seem…distracted tonight.

Are you having second thoughts about the two of us being seen together publicly?"

Georgia shook her head. She had a lot on her mind, but surprisingly, the budding romance between her and Carson was not one of her worries. "No, no. I'm sorry. I've just got a lot on my mind tonight."

Carson nodded and picked up his wine. His plate was empty and the server came by to take it away. Georgia let him take hers, as well. She didn't have much of an appetite and hadn't since she'd gotten that phone call. The universe had basically ground to a halt at that moment, but no one seemed to notice but her.

"Want to talk about it? I'm all ears," he said, taking a sip of his wine.

She was almost afraid to talk about what had happened out loud, but she did want to share it with someone. Carson was the only person she'd told about her past, and he might really understand what was going on and how important it was. The only other person she could tell was her former caseworker, Sheila. She'd avoided that call, however. Somehow she worried Sheila wouldn't think this was a great development.

"Okay," she agreed. "Well, yesterday evening, I got a phone call. From my mother."

Carson perked up in his seat. "Your mother? Really?"

Georgia nodded. "I could hardly believe it myself. I've gone twenty-six years without her in my life, and then all of a sudden, she calls me out of nowhere. She said she saw my news conference about the hospital last week and hunted down my number to get in contact with me."

"That must've been quite a shock."

"You have no idea." She'd actually been in tears. She held it together as long as she could, but once she hung up the phone, she'd bawled like a baby for twenty minutes. It was so surreal to pick up the phone and hear the voice of someone claiming to be her mother. She didn't even remember what her mother's voice sounded like, but it didn't take long to figure out she really was talking to Misty Lynn Adams.

"What did she say?"

"Well, it wasn't a long call, but she said she was getting her life back together and wanted to reconnect with me. I get the feeling this is part of a recovery program she's in to stay clean and sober. She wants to come to Chicago and see me."

"Wow," Carson said, reaching across the table to take Georgia's hand. "That's really great. How do you feel about all this?"

That was the difference between telling this story to someone who grew up with both parents and telling someone like Carson, who knew what it was like to live without knowing your past. Anyone else would've asked if she was excited and happy. Those weren't quite the words for it. Cautious was more like it. Hopeful, but not too much. Being hurt as many times as she had made her loath to jump in with both feet, but she was going to try.

"It's a mix of emotions," she admitted. "I want to see her and ask her some questions, but I don't think we're about to be best friends or anything. That's going to take time, if it's even possible. My mother is pretty messed up. I don't know how long she's had her act together, but if she relapses, I don't want to get caught in it."

Carson nodded sympathetically. "I understand. You want to know your family and have that relationship, but there's a reason why they haven't been in your life. Sometimes you wonder if it isn't for the best."

"Exactly. But I'm going to meet with her. I sent her some money to take the bus here from Detroit and she's going to stay with me for a few days. We'll see what happens."

At her words, Carson frowned. He was silent as he watched her face for a moment. "Georgia," he said at last, "is giving her money a good idea? And letting her stay with you? She's a virtual stranger."

She tugged her hand from his and buried it under the table. "I've thought of all that. It was only a hundred dollars for the bus ticket. If she blows it on drugs and never shows up, it was a relatively cheap lesson learned. But I have to have a little bit of faith if this is going to work."

"But staying with you," he pressed. "I don't think that's a good idea."

What little enthusiasm Georgia had about this development with her mother was starting to wane in the face of Carson's skepticism. What did he want Georgia to do? Hide the good silver? She didn't have good silver. Most of her money had gone into her loft and that was one thing her mother couldn't take, no matter how hard she tried.

"What are my choices? If she can't afford a bus ticket, she can't afford a hotel. I'd have to pay for it, too. It's only for a few days, Carson. If I feel remotely uncomfortable having her there, or leaving her there alone, I'll get her a room somewhere, okay?"

Carson flinched at her sharp, defensive tone. "Listen, I'm sorry to be such a pessimist, Georgia, but I guess it's just a by-product of how I grew up. I just don't want you to get hurt."

"I won't," she insisted. "I know I have to tread carefully with Misty, but I could use your support. I've encouraged your search for your father, and I'd really appreciate your support as I look into my own past."

Carson got up from his side of the restaurant booth and sat down beside her. He wrapped her in a hug and kissed her sweetly on the cheek. "I support you one hundred percent. Don't ever doubt that. I'm just worried about you, is all."

Georgia eased into his embrace, letting her anxieties fade away in his arms. She supposed he was right to feel cautious about the whole thing. There wasn't much point in jumping to Misty's defense when she knew nothing about her. "Well, thank you. I'm not used to anyone worrying about me."

"You'd better get used to it, although I'll admit I could be just a little on edge after what Graham found. My mom had warned us that our father was a terrible person, but I never could've imagined that it could be Sutton Winchester. Of all the men in Chicago…"

Georgia had been quite stunned to hear the news herself. After he told her the rest of the story, it had made sense. Carson had Sutton's mischievous green eyes, but she didn't want to tell him that. At this point, she got the feeling he didn't want to have anything in common with Sutton, especially common genetics. "What are you guys going to do?"

"Graham is going to try to track down someone who might remember the two of them being together back then. If we're successful, we'll push for a paternity test to know once and for all."

Georgia nodded absently as he described their plans, but she could tell the brothers had little idea what they would do with the truth. "So if he is your father, then what?"

As she predicted, Carson frowned slightly. "I don't know. I doubt we'll be invited over for Thanksgiving dinner with his other children. If we play any role in his life, we're going to have to fight for it. I think Graham and Brooks are more willing to battle than I am. I just keep thinking of my mother's warnings. She kept him out of our lives for a reason. All things considered, do you really want him in my life?"

Georgia nodded. "I know I'm taking a risk by letting my mother come see me. It might work out, or she might be the same junkie who abandoned me. I've done pretty well without her. At the same time, I won't let myself give up on her. With your parents, you stand there and let yourself get kicked in the teeth again and again in the hope that they will finally stand up and be the people you always dreamed of. That child in you is always craving that love and acceptance you didn't get. If you give up on that, what's left?"

"Everything else," Carson argued. "Your mother was a broke, messed up kid who had no business taking care of a baby, but Sutton is the richest guy in Chicago. What's his excuse? Sutton knows that we're his kids. He hasn't once sought us out in all these years. No birthday cards, no child support, not even a little lenience in business dealings. Why would I want a man like that in my life?"

"You won't know for sure until you get to know him better."

"I've never had a father, Georgia. I don't know

whether it's better to have a lousy one and know the truth than to never have one and always wonder."

"I understand. With the truth come things you may not want to know. I'm giving my mother this chance, but considering my father impregnated a teenage runaway with a drug problem, I think I'll go with never knowing him. That way I can keep the fantasy father in my mind. I'd rather not know than find out he was her customer, or her drug dealer, or that he raped a young girl with no one to turn to."

Carson carefully considered her words and then took the final sip of his wine. "Well, in the end I don't get to make the decision, because there's more than just me in the equation. My brothers want to see this through no matter what. Like it or not, I will know if Sutton is my father. As for what comes after that… I guess that all depends on dear old Dad."

Georgia nodded and finished her drink. They were both in limbo when it came to their parents. She hated that feeling. For years, as she bounced from one foster home to the next, she had both hoped and worried that her mother would get her act together and take her home for good.

She had been excited about her mother seeking her out. She had made the first step, which is something Georgia had been adamant about. It wouldn't have taken much to track down her mother, but she didn't want to. Knowing that her mother had gone to the trouble of finding her felt good. Still, she was scared. And after talking to Carson about Misty's visit, she wasn't feeling as optimistic.

Georgia could already tell that she would spend all night lying in bed worrying about this. Her mother was due to arrive on Friday, so that meant days of anxiety until she knew for certain. She needed a distraction. Something to keep her mind off the situation. Work wouldn't do it, but leaning into Carson's chest and resting her head on his shoulder gave her a good idea of what might.

"Are you ready to get out of here?" she asked.

"I thought you wanted dessert."

Reaching up to caress his stubble-covered jaw, Georgia turned his head until his full lips met with hers. She drank him in, letting her tongue curl along his as she gave a soft moan of approval. A sizzle of awareness traveled down her spine, making her suddenly warm and flush in the previously cold restaurant. All thoughts of Misty and Sutton faded away with his touch.

She was right. Losing herself in a night of passion with Carson was just what she needed. What they both needed. "I do," she said as she pulled away and looked into his eyes with wicked intention.

"Then let's go." Carson smiled wide and scanned the bill the waiter had brought. He tossed some cash on the table for it and slipped out of the booth with Georgia's hand in his own.

Seven

"Rebecca, what is this three o'clock on my calendar today?" Carson waited impatiently for his assistant to answer him as he studied his computer screen. He hadn't made this appointment, and he had no real clue who the woman was that he and his brothers were scheduled to meet in just a few minutes' time.

Rebecca appeared in the doorway and shook her head. "I'm not really sure, sir. Graham called this morning and told me to add it. Did he not speak with you?"

No, he had not. But Carson didn't want to worry Rebecca. "He may have and I just forgot. Thank you."

Rebecca slipped back out of his office, leaving him to ponder the appointment. He didn't have long to wait. Brooks showed up a few minutes later, eyeing his smart phone with dismay. "What's the three o'clock about?"

Carson shrugged. "It's Graham's doing. He didn't tell you, either?"

"Why would he do something like that?" Brooks flopped down into Carson's guest chair and frowned. "Who is Tammy Ross? I've never heard of her."

"She is Sutton Winchester's retired housekeeper." Graham appeared in the doorway with a smug grin on his face.

That was the last thing Carson expected. Why would they be meeting with Sutton's old housekeeper, unless… "Does she know anything about Sutton's relationship with our mother?"

Graham strolled at an obnoxiously slow pace across the Moroccan rug and sat down in the other chair. "She does."

"Why not just tell us what she had to say? Why bring her here?"

"Because," Graham insisted, "she wanted to talk to all of us in person. Apparently she feels bad about how it all went down back then. She's a sentimental older lady who knew and liked our mother. Indulge her a little."

"Mr. Newport," Carson's assistant chirped through the speaker phone. "Mrs. Ross is here to see you."

"Right on time," Graham said with a smile. He got up from his chair and went to the reception area. A moment later he returned with a petite older woman with short gray hair and a pleasant smile.

Carson and Brooks both stood to greet their guest. "Mrs. Ross," Carson said, reaching out to shake her hand. "Please have a seat." He gestured over to his conference table and followed the others there as they took their seats.

"Thank you for seeing me today. When Graham contacted me and I realized I was talking to one of the twins all grown up—" the woman's dark eyes grew a little misty "—well, I knew I had to tell you everything I knew. My loyalty to the Winchesters ended with the paychecks."

"I contacted the agency that Sutton hires household staff through," Graham explained. "I was able to talk to someone and they passed along my number to her."

"I read about your mother's passing in the paper," she said. "It was hard to believe that the vibrant young girl I knew was gone. Or that the babies I remembered were full-grown men."

"How did you know about our mother?" Brooks asked.

"At first I knew Cynthia as Mr. Sutton's secretary. She would call the house from time to time relaying his requests for dinner or telling me what shirt he wanted starched for the next day. She was sweet and we chatted some. She was very excited about her pregnancy, and having two children of my own, I relayed plenty of advice. After the twins—*you*—were born, I volunteered to babysit a couple of nights while she went out. I didn't realize at the time who she was going out with or whose babies I was watching."

"So our mother *was* seeing Sutton on the side?"

"Yes. From what I gathered, they were together long before she started working at Elite Industries. It wasn't surprising, though. Your mother was a lovely young woman, just the kind Sutton liked. I think his marriage to Celeste Van Houten was more business than pleasure, so he was always on the prowl for… extracurricular entertainment."

Carson's stomach ached to think of his mother as just one in a line of women who had marched in and out of Sutton Winchester's bedroom. She deserved better. A real love with a man who wanted to marry her and give her all the happiness in the world. Instead she'd raised his three children alone on a waitress's salary. Carson wasn't sure what their mother would've done without Gerty's help.

"Finding out about you was the biggest shock," Mrs. Ross said, looking at Carson. "Your mother must have left the company so soon into her second pregnancy that I didn't even know she was expecting again. I'm sure that was part of Mr. Winchester's plan. Mrs. Winchester was already beside herself over the relationship. I don't think she knew about the twins, and I'm sure Mr. Winchester didn't want anyone to know about you, either."

"If he was so secretive, how do you know about all of this?"

The older woman smiled. "There are different kinds of rich people and in my day, I worked for them all. The Winchesters are the kind of rich people who see their employees as a lesser species. Sometimes Mrs. Winchester pretended I wasn't even there. Or maybe she wasn't pretending. Maybe I just wasn't important enough for her notice. It was annoying, but sometimes it was useful.

"I remember one night Mr. and Mrs. Winchester really got into a row. She was pregnant with Nora at the time. Mrs. Winchester didn't yell much, but it was a glass-breaking night. They went into the bedroom and closed the door, but it didn't matter. You could hear them yelling from anywhere in the house, and the house is a mansion. I was in the hallway, sweeping up a glass vase she'd thrown at him, when I heard her mention Cynthia's name. She told him she wasn't just going to sit by and let him parade around with his secretary while she was suffering through another difficult pregnancy to have his child. She threatened to divorce him and clean him out. She told him he'd never see Eve or the new baby again. I had no doubt she could do it. Her brother was one of the most ruthless divorce attorneys in Illinois. She told him he would end it, or she would end him.

"It was then I realized that the twins had to be his. I couldn't imagine Mr. Winchester taking care of a woman with another man's children the way he did. A week later, a lady called the house claiming to be Mr. Winchester's secretary. When I asked what happened to Cynthia, she told me that she was no longer with the company. That's the last I heard of her, or of any of you. She disappeared after that."

"You can't be certain that I'm Sutton's child, though," Carson said. "She could've gotten pregnant by someone else after she left Elite."

The older woman reached across the table and patted his hand. "You are Sutton Winchester's boy, no doubt in my mind. Your brothers take more after Cynthia, but you, you're the spitting image of your father when he was younger."

Carson swallowed hard. He'd always known he looked different from his brothers and likely took after their father while they favored their mother, but he didn't want to be the spitting *anything* of Sutton Winchester.

"Mrs. Ross, would you be willing to testify to a judge about what you told us today?" Graham asked. "Odds are that it won't be necessary for us to compel the paternity test, but the judge might ask to speak with you."

"Absolutely. I think I've stayed quiet about all this long enough. Mr. Winchester needs to do right by his children. It's never too late for that."

"Thank you for coming to speak with us today," Carson said, shaking the woman's hand.

She took it, standing up and clutching her bag to her side. "It was no trouble. I've wondered for years what happened to Cynthia's babies. Now I know. She would be so proud of you three. I'm sure of it."

Graham escorted the woman out of the office, returning about ten minutes later. "So? What do you think?"

"I think you're the luckiest bastard in the world," Brooks said. "I can't fathom how you managed to find her."

"Luck has nothing to do with it," he said, dropping into a chair. "Law school is brutal, but it teaches you how to find the information you need to sway the court in your favor. My research skills are second to none. It wasn't easy, I assure you. I called every damn employment agency in town before I struck gold. If that hadn't worked, I was going to try to smooth-talk his accountant into finding past employment records. Thankfully, this worked."

"So now what?" Carson asked.

"I've got the paperwork all ready to submit to the judge," Graham said. "Once he issues the order for the paternity test, we'll deliver it to Sutton. When we're certain he's our father, we'll make our bid to be included in his estate, sit back and watch the fireworks."

"I knew you'd be back."

Georgia ignored Sutton's smug expression. It was far more unnerving to look him in the eye now that she recognized that those green eyes were so much like Carson's. Knowing this man was likely Carson's father was hard to stomach, especially when his gaze raked over her with poorly masked desire.

"Does Newport know you're here?"

"No, he doesn't." Georgia hadn't told him because she knew Carson wouldn't let her do this. She wanted to keep the door open to Sutton. Not because she wanted the job, but because she wanted information. If Carson and his brothers ended up taking Sutton to court, anything she came up with could be helpful. And if she could get some money for the hospital from him, more the better.

"So have you come to your senses and decided to accept my offer? Finally figure out Newport isn't man enough for you?"

She tried not to roll her eyes. She needed to play along, at least for a little bit, if she was going to get what she wanted out of this meeting. Georgia knew it was dangerous to waltz back into the lion's den, but it was the only way to get the information she was after.

"A girl has to keep her options open."

Sutton's chuckle was punctuated with a long bout of coughing. He pulled the pocket square from his suit coat and held it over his mouth. She couldn't help but notice as she watched him that he didn't look well. His suit was hanging off him. His face was slightly sunken in, emphasizing his cheekbones and the gray circles beneath his eyes. He seemed to have deteriorated pretty rapidly since she saw him at the party about a week ago.

When he finished coughing and pulled the handkerchief away, Georgia noticed a few small droplets of blood on the fabric. Sutton was seriously ill. He didn't need a mistress. He needed a doctor.

"I think I could use a drink." Sutton cleared his throat, pushed up from his desk and walked over to the minibar in the corner. "Can I get you something?"

"Sure." Standing up, she followed Sutton to where he was dropping ice cubes into two crystal tumblers. She leaned against the edge of the conference room table and watched as he poured himself some scotch, and then made her a vodka gimlet. It was her favorite drink, although she had no idea how he could possibly know that.

Finally he held up her glass to her. "Here you go, my dear. What shall we drink to?"

Georgia eyed the glass until she came up with an answer. "To keeping our options open," she said with a smile.

"Indeed." He clinked his crystal against hers and took a sip. He watched her as she drank some of her drink, then set his glass down on the edge of the table beside her. "So what is it that I can do for you today, Georgia? Are you ready to accept my generous offer?"

"Not yet."

"Well, 'not yet' is better than the no you gave me last time. I'm making progress."

Georgia was willing to let a sickly old man believe that if it made him feel better. "It's a woman's prerogative to change her mind."

"Never were truer words spoken." Sutton took a step toward her, crowding into her space and leaning close. "What would convince you to accept my offer, Georgia? Just name it. More money? Jewelry? A nice high-rise penthouse? I can give you anything you want if you'll give yourself to me right now." His hand rested on her thigh as he gazed intently at her. She got the feeling he meant it. But there was no way she would accept.

"I'll have to think on that," she said as she picked up his hand and moved it off her leg. "But there are some things you could do that might sway my final decision."

"A negotiator, eh? I'll bite." He scooped up his drink, although he didn't move away. They were nearly touching. "Like what?"

"I'd like Elite Industries to make a donation to the Newport children's hospital project."

He narrowed his gaze at her as he sipped his scotch. "And why would I want to do that?"

"Well, I happen to know that you don't have a public relations director at the moment. If I were heading up your PR department, that is exactly what

I would recommend. People know that you were competing for the land where the hospital will be built. Some may think that Elite should've backed down on the condo project to support a worthy cause. I think donating to the hospital would be good damage control."

"I don't need damage control. I run this town."

"That may be," she continued, "but you wouldn't want to look like a poor sport for losing to Newport, would you? I know you're not used to losing, so you might not know how to handle it."

"Losing…" Sutton muttered. "If I had wanted that land, I would've gotten it."

He could tell himself that, but he'd passed along his stubbornness to Carson along with his eyes. "Sure you would've," she agreed. "But what better way to bless the project you let happen than by supporting it? Come on, Sutton. Just cut a check."

Sutton leaned into her, forcing Georgia to lean farther back on the conference room table. "And aside from good PR, what will my check get me?"

Georgia placed a hand on Sutton's chest to keep him from moving any closer. "That depends on how big the check is."

A wide grin spread across the older man's face, suddenly reminding her so much of Carson that her chest ached. "You're a feisty one. I love that about you. You win. I'll write a check to Newport for whatever you want."

"Write it for however much you think I'm worth."

"Mr. Winchester? Georgia?" A sharp, startled voice sounded from the other side of the office.

Georgia snapped her head to the door of Sutton's office, where Graham was standing. His face showed a mix of surprise and anger as he looked at the two of them together. Hovering over his shoulder was Eve Winchester, the oldest of Sutton's three daughters and corporate heir apparent. Both of them looked quite stunned to walk in on Sutton nearly manhandling Georgia.

"I'm sorry, Daddy," Eve said. "I couldn't stop him."

Georgia pressed harder against Sutton's chest and he finally backed away. With a sigh, he turned away from Georgia to address the interlopers in his office. "It's no problem. I've got Newport employees all over the place today. Come in, come in."

Sutton strolled back over to his desk, and Georgia tried to pull herself back together. She was hardly misbehaving, but she didn't like the look on Graham's face. He obviously thought he was walking in on something. Georgia avoided his gaze, holding her position near the conference room table.

"What can I do for you, Graham? Or are you Brooks? Damn it, I can never tell you two apart."

That made Graham angry. His jaw tightened and the edges of his ears reddened as he stared Sutton down. "You'd think that a father would be able to tell his own children apart."

Sutton barely reacted to the accusation. He leaned back in his chair and laced his fingers together over his stomach. "A father *would*, but I'm not sure I like what you're implying, Mr. Newport."

"I'm implying nothing. I'm saying it straight up, *Dad*."

Georgia held her breath as she watched the two men speak. The tension in the room was thick. Her gaze drifted over to Eve. She'd followed Graham into the office and seemed to be the only one in the room stunned by Graham's accusations. And if Georgia was reading her correctly, Eve looked a bit disappointed, too. She supposed any red-blooded woman in Chicago would feel the same way if she found out the handsome and rich Newport boys were her half brothers.

"I am not your father." Sutton didn't hesitate to shoot down Graham.

"Are you denying you had a relationship with my mother?"

Sutton pursed his lips, considering his response. "I did have a relationship with Cynthia. She was a lovely woman. You take after her, I have to admit. But I am not your father. Your mother was already pregnant when we met."

Graham laid an envelope on Sutton's desk. "We'll see about that."

Sutton opened the envelope and pulled out the paperwork inside. "A subpoena for a paternity test?

That's cute. Very well," he said, setting the paperwork aside. "I will comply with the court order. But
don't get cocky thinking you've won some kind of
battle here, Graham. In the end, you won't like the
results, because I am not your father."

Graham started down Sutton without flinching. "I
wouldn't expect a man like you to say anything else."

Graham turned his attention to Georgia on the far
side of the room. "Do you need a ride back to the office?" His tone was pointed, but she wasn't surprised.

"I do." She'd gotten what she wanted out of Sutton
for now. Staying behind after this incident would be
nothing but awkward for them both.

Moving quickly, she scooped up her big black
purse and slung it over her shoulder. Not wanting
to let things unravel with Sutton, she gave him one
last smile before she followed Graham out of the office. "Can you have that check for the hospital sent
by courier over to our offices?"

The irritation faded from Sutton's eyes as he focused on her again. "I'll have it taken care of."

Turning, she caught Graham and Eve sharing
a meaningful look. Interesting. She brushed past
a stunned Eve on her way to meet Graham in the
doorway. They were halfway to his car before he
said anything to her.

"What was that about?" he asked.

She didn't like the way he was addressing her, as
though he'd caught her beneath Sutton's desk. "I've

got a better question," she said, deflecting the discussion. "What exactly was that just now between you and Eve Winchester?"

Graham's jaw stiffened, but he didn't turn to look at her. Instead he held open the door to the parking garage. "That was nothing."

Georgia laughed. She didn't work much with Graham since he spent so much time at his law firm, but she knew enough to know he was lying. "Tell that to someone who believes you. Eve was watching you like a tasty meal. At least until you started calling her father 'Dad.'"

Graham took a deep breath and pulled his keys from his pocket. "If Sutton is our father, then it doesn't matter what you think you saw. This isn't a V.C. Andrews novel. The odds are that Eve is my half sister, so end of story."

He opened the car door and Georgia slipped inside. Once he got in and started the engine, she said, "Sutton seemed pretty adamant that he wasn't your father."

"Yes, well, did you expect otherwise?"

Georgia hesitated for a moment. That didn't sound like Sutton's style. Maybe he would lie by omission, but the way he insisted he wasn't Graham's father made her believe him. Her interactions with him had always been very direct. "I don't know. I've never known him to lie. He usually gets his way without stooping to deceit."

"You know him so well now, do you? How much time have you been spending here with him behind Carson's back? He told me about the dirty old man's offer. Have you changed your mind about accepting it?"

"No, I haven't. We were talking business." She refused to elaborate any further. It was none of his damn business what she was doing there anyway.

"I bet," he snapped before shooting into traffic and tearing down the street. "Let me give you a word of advice about Carson. He doesn't get involved with women very often. His last real relationship ended when the woman dumped him for a richer guy."

Georgia didn't know that. They hadn't really discussed their dating history in depth. "Really?"

"Yes. He and Candy were even engaged when she decided to run off with some billionaire tech innovator. It was really hard on him."

"Well, Carson and I are just—"

"I don't care what you two are or aren't," Graham interrupted. "I just want you to know so you think long and hard about putting Carson through the same thing again."

Georgia bit her tongue. She was about as far from leaving Carson for Sutton as she was from leaving him for Prince Harry. She wasn't going to argue that point with Graham. She'd tell Carson what she was up to, but she didn't think Graham could be trusted. Judging by the body language between him and Eve, he was compromised. Especially if Sutton wasn't their father.

If either of them was going to be sleeping with the enemy, it was Graham.

Eight

"Can we talk?" Carson caught Georgia as she went past him in the hallway.

"Let me grab something off the printer," she said, "and then I'll come by."

Carson returned to his office. He was filled with nervous energy that wouldn't let him sit. Instead he stood and looked out the window at the sprawling sights of downtown Chicago. The view he loved did little to soothe him. He'd been tied up in knots inside since Graham left his office earlier.

His brother's tale of the meeting with Sutton and Georgia's unexpected presence had left him with a number of questions. He wasn't sure he would like the answers. The dread in his stomach felt so familiar.

He didn't want to believe what Graham implied about Georgia, and he fought to reserve judgment no matter how badly his instincts wanted to react. Then again, he'd felt the same way when he'd started hearing the rumors about his ex-fiancée, Candy, stepping out with another man. He hadn't wanted to believe it at first and yet the nagging ache in his gut couldn't be ignored.

Breaking off their engagement hadn't really bothered him. If Carson were honest with himself, he hadn't been in love with Candy Stratton. She had been convenient—everything he thought a good wife should be. He didn't have the time to look around forever, so he'd decided to move forward with her.

What had gutted him, though, was why Candy left him. He'd done well for himself. He and his brothers had crawled their way up from an unremarkable start in life to be some of the wealthiest and most successful businessmen in Chicago. Carson was painfully aware that he wasn't from a good family. That he was a bastard, unclaimed by his father. He already had a daily battle shoring up his feelings of self-worth and adequacy.

What he didn't need was a woman ditching him for a man who had all the things he lacked. For a while he'd wondered if he'd ever be enough. He had a ton of money, but not enough for Candy. He was very successful, but not successful enough for his father to be proud and step forward to claim his son. No matter how hard he worked, it never seemed like enough.

He'd hoped he could be enough for Georgia. A lot had changed since his engagement—he was wiser, older and even more successful. And yet it felt the same. Would it be that much worse if Georgia ditched him for his own father?

"You wanted to speak with me?"

Carson turned to find Georgia at the threshold. "Yes. Please come in. Shut the door and have a seat."

Georgia narrowed her gaze at him for a moment before complying. "Is this about yesterday?" she asked, sitting down.

Carson took a seat behind his desk and sighed. "Maybe. I had a discussion with Graham this morning that wasn't very encouraging, but I'd like to hear your version of events."

"It's not a version of events. Graham has no idea what he walked in on."

"What did he walk in on?" After the way his brother described it, he wasn't entirely sure he wanted to hear it from her own lips. The thought of her getting involved with his father was enough to make him want to punch a hole through his office wall.

"Nothing more than a little corporate espionage."

Carson's brow shot up. "What?"

"Listen," Georgia said, sitting forward in her seat. "With everything going on between Newport Corporation and Elite Industries, I decided it was a good idea to keep the lines of communication open. If Sutton thought I was still considering his offer, I might be able to get some information from him that could help you. There's nothing more to it than that."

Carson breathed a deep sigh of relief. He hadn't realized he'd been holding his breath for so long. He tried to suppress the doubts in his mind that Candy had left behind. There was no real reason to doubt Georgia. He needed to at least try to hear her out and see if he could trust her. "Really?"

Georgia got up from her seat. She rounded his desk and settled into his lap. She ran her fingers through his hair and looked down at him with her pale gray eyes. "Yes, really. Would you like to know what I've found out so far?"

She already had information? That was faster than he expected. At the same time, the weight of her firm, round behind in his lap was sending his thoughts in another direction. He settled for resting a hand on her bare knee and stroking her soft skin. "Sure, tell me."

"Well, first I secured a large donation from Elite for the children's hospital. Sutton will be having a check sent over by courier this week."

Carson couldn't help the smile that spread across his face. He wrapped his arms around Georgia and pulled her soft body tight against his own. She was an amazing woman, and for some reason, she wanted to be with him. "Really?"

"Yep. I don't think his pride will let him donate

less than seven figures so he can always have top billing on the list of corporate sponsors. I also have some interesting personal information about Sutton that you and your brothers might need to know."

Personal information? "Like what?" he asked.

"Graham wasn't there long enough to notice this, but I was. I think Sutton is sick."

"Sick? That old bastard is too mean to get sick. The germs are repelled by him."

Georgia didn't smile at his joke. "I'm serious, Carson. I'm not talking about him having a cold here. He was coughing up blood. He's lost weight. He looks terrible. He does a good job trying to hide it, but I really think something is wrong with him."

If what she said was true, it wasn't public knowledge. The failing health of the King of Chicago would start wild speculation. Who would take over Elite Industries? Who were the beneficiaries of his will? How many of his mistresses would show up at the funeral?

Ideally, those paternity-test results would come through quickly. They were running short on time if Graham and Brooks were dead set on getting their piece of the Winchester pie. Sooner was better than later. If they *were* Sutton's children, pushing their way into the will once he announced he was ill would look really bad. While Carson didn't care much for appearances, the last thing he wanted was for people to think he was a ruthless chip off the old block.

That was just his luck, though. He'd gone over thirty years wondering who his father was. Within days of finding a solid candidate, the man got sick. If Georgia was right and this was a serious illness, just how long would he have with dear ol' Dad before he died? Not long enough, although Carson doubted they'd have a touching, father-son bonding moment even if Sutton lived for another decade.

"Carson? Are you okay?" Georgia asked.

He realized he hadn't responded to her revelations. "I'm fine. I guess I was trying to think through what all that would mean for us. Do you really think he's seriously ill?"

Georgia shrugged. "I'm no doctor, but he looked bad to me. This wasn't the flu or a passing stomach bug. Whatever has hit him, has hit him hard and taken a physical toll quickly."

"Well, the man does have a reputation for hard living. Perhaps it's catching up with him."

Georgia studied his face for a moment, and then ran her finger along his jaw. "Are you still mad at me for going over to meet with Sutton?"

"No, I'm not mad. I'm actually pleased by your underhandedness."

"Do you want me to stop going over there?"

Carson considered her question. He should say yes, but she was right. There was valuable information to be had. "No. Keep visiting him if you think it's useful and you feel comfortable around him. Just be careful. That guy can't be trusted."

"I think he's more talk than action these days, but I promise to tell you if I go back. But you know you don't have to worry about me leaving you for him, right? It doesn't matter what he offers. I'm not going to run off with Winchester."

She looked at Carson with her big gray eyes and he had no choice but to believe her. She wasn't Candy and despite what Graham thought he saw, nothing was happening with Sutton. If she'd wanted to leave him for the old man, she would've done it when he first offered the job. Instead she was here, sitting in Carson's lap, telling him she wasn't going anywhere. That was the sexiest thing she could've said to him.

"I'd like to think so," he said, "but we've only been together a little less than two weeks. We're hardly serious enough for me to start making demands on you."

"You can make a few demands," she said coyly. "I like a man who's in charge. At least in the bedroom."

Georgia shifted on his lap, and all thoughts of his potential father's potential illness vanished. He wanted to hike up the hem of her skirt, brush his fingertips across her bare thighs and take her on his desk. The fantasy played out so vividly in his mind that he had to squirm uncomfortably beneath her to avoid his building arousal pressing inappropriately into her. He was breaking a pretty sensible rule by having a relationship with one of his employees. He wasn't going to compound the problem and blur the lines by making love to Georgia here.

Instead he palmed the curve of her rear end through her pencil skirt and gave her a wicked look. "Is it time to go home yet?"

She smiled and looked at his desk clock. "It's only three thirty."

"Yes, but I'm the boss. When the boss says you can go home early, you can go home early."

Leaning in, Georgia pressed her lips to his, lighting the fire in his belly that quickly rushed through his veins. "Whatever you say, Mr. Newport."

Georgia stood waiting anxiously outside the bus station. Tonight was the night her mother was arriving from Detroit. She had texted to let her know she made her connection and would be arriving at six thirty. A steady stream of people had started coming out of the station. Glancing down at her phone, Georgia confirmed it was almost 6:45. Her mother could be the next person to step out the door.

Her nerves were getting the best of her. This was a big moment for her. She didn't know how it was going to go. Carson's skepticism had planted seeds of doubt in her mind, but she was trying hard not to cultivate them. She was too scared to have big dreams about her fantasy mother and their new relationship, but she desperately wanted something with her.

Just then, a woman came out the front door. She was a blonde, in her early forties. She had a backpack slung over one shoulder and a small duffel bag in one hand. Her hair was pulled back in a ponytail and her clothes were wrinkled from hours traveling on a bus.

When their eyes met, Georgia knew that it was her mother. She was surprised to find she looked so young. Misty had been a teenager when she had Georgia, but in her mind, she had envisioned her mother being older somehow.

"Georgia?" the woman asked, stopping a few feet away.

"Hi, Mom." She didn't know what else to say.

The woman approached her cautiously. It seemed both of them were at a loss for how to handle this momentous event. Finally she dropped her duffel bag on the ground and lunged forward to wrap her daughter in a hug.

Georgia buried her face in her mother's neck and hung on. She could feel the sting of tears in her eyes and hid them by letting them spill onto her mother's sweater.

"Oh, my li'l Peaches," her mother whispered as they continued to embrace. "Let me get a good look at you."

They separated so Misty could study her daughter's face. Georgia tried not to squirm under the scrutiny, focusing instead on the realization that her mother was really here.

"You turned out to be so beautiful," Misty said. "I was a pretty girl, but you…you are the most stunning woman I've ever seen in real life. Like a movie star."

"Hardly," Georgia said, awkwardly dismissing her praise.

"And you've done so well for yourself. Such nice clothes, so well-groomed. Seeing you on the news working for that big real estate development company… I was so proud."

"Thank you." Georgia was never comfortable with how she looked, but she'd worked hard for her success and would accept those compliments while she dismissed others. "Are you hungry? I thought maybe we could get some dinner."

"You know, I'm really just tired from all the traveling. Would you mind too much if we just went back to your place and got some food delivered?"

Georgia smiled. Perhaps she had gotten her love of takeout from her mother without knowing it. "That would be fine. There's a great Chinese place near my house, or an Italian eatery around the block."

"I love Chinese," Misty said with a smile and picked up her duffel bag.

That must be genetic, too.

"So, where are you parked?" Misty asked, looking around the parking lot.

"Oh, I don't have a car. I stay in the city, so I usually ride the train." Misty's disappointed expression caught her off guard. Georgia quickly realized that she was probably tired and not really interested in navigating any more public transportation today. "But I can get a taxi," she added.

The smile returned to Misty's face. "That would be wonderful. I got hit by a drunk driver a few years ago and shattered my pelvis," she said, shuffling from one foot to the other. "I can't stay on my feet for too long or it aches."

Georgia's eyes widened. She didn't even know how to respond. Instead she called for a taxi, and they rode back to her apartment in relative silence. Once they stepped out of the cab, she could tell that Misty was in a state of awe. She looked up at the tall building Georgia called home as though they were about to step into a lush European castle. They walked through the nicely appointed lobby with Misty seeming unsure quite where to look. The marble floors? The shining brass elevator doors? The giant floral arrangement at the front desk?

"I don't think I've ever been anyplace this nice before," Misty said as they entered Georgia's apartment. Her gaze ran over the pieces of art on the walls and the entire wall of windows on the one side that overlooked the Chicago cityscape. "I'm afraid to touch anything," she said, clutching anxiously at her backpack.

"There's nothing to worry about. Just put down your things and relax." Georgia took her duffel bag and set it in the living room by the couch. "Unfortunately I don't have a guest room. I've never actually had a guest, so we'll have to make up the sofa bed for you."

"Okay. It's nice of you to let me stay with you at all. Hopefully it doesn't aggravate my back condition."

"What happened to your back?"

Misty sighed. "Honey, after the life I've lived, there's something wrong with every part of me. You don't want to hear my sob stories. You've got plenty of your own, thanks to me, I'm sure."

"No, really," Georgia pressed. It was hard not knowing anything about her mother aside from what was in her file. "What happened?"

She put her backpack on the ground and crossed her arms protectively over her chest. The movement pushed up the sleeves of her shirt, exposing a sad collage of scars across her pale skin. "About ten years ago my dealer had his thugs come for me because I owed him money. They pushed me down the stairs at my apartment complex. They had to put some screws and pins in my spine, so I have trouble sleeping sometimes."

"That's terrible."

Misty just shrugged it away. "Like I said, you don't want to hear about my life. I'm sure there's a part of you that hates me, and I don't blame you for that. But being taken away from me was probably the best thing that ever happened to you. I'm pretty sure that anyone else would've been a better parent than I was. That's why I never…" She hesitated, her face flushing red with emotion. "That's why I never tried to get you back. I thought you were better off without me. And I was right. Just look at you now. You'd be a mess like me if I'd fought to get you back. That's why I let all of you go."

Georgia swallowed hard. She had grown up thinking her mother had never cared for her. From the sound of it, the opposite was true. Her mother had stayed out of her life *because* she cared. Part of what she'd said confused her, though. "What do you mean, all of us?"

Misty's gaze dropped to the floor. "You have a younger brother and a sister, Georgia. I should've told you that before."

Georgia was nearly blown off her feet. A brother and a sister? All this time she'd thought she was alone in the world, and now she found out she had siblings she never knew about? "Where? Tell me about them."

"There's not much I can tell you. I'm sorry. I was so drug addicted by then that they took the babies from me right after each of them was born. They were both adopted, so I don't know their names or where they ended up. I might have been messed up, but by then I knew giving up my rights would allow them to have a real family and not end up in the foster system like you. I should've done the same for you, but they told me it was harder to place an older child. By then you were five or six. I've got a lot of sins to pay for," Misty said.

Georgia's knees grew weak beneath her, and she slipped down into the nearby armchair before she fell. She'd known she would learn a lot about her mother and her early years with her, but somehow she hadn't anticipated this.

"I'm sorry for that, Peaches. I'm sorry for all of this. That's why I wanted to come here, to see you. To tell you how bad I feel about everything that happened in your life. It's a part of my recovery, one step at a time. I don't expect you to forgive me, but I needed to come anyway."

"I think we've got a lot of talking to do while you're here," Georgia managed.

"That we do." Turning away, Misty patted the cushions of the couch. "I think this will be comfortable enough. It's a really nice couch. It's got to be better than the cot at the shelter."

Georgia felt a pang of guilt for putting her mother on the couch. She got to sleep in a nice bed every night; she should let her mother do it while she was here. "You know what, Mom? Why don't you take my bed upstairs? It's a nice memory foam bed, so you'll be comfortable. I can sleep down here."

"Oh no," Misty argued. "I didn't tell you all that to make you feel bad."

"Really. It's not a problem. Let's take your things upstairs and I can show you around."

Her mother followed her upstairs to the loft bedroom that overlooked the living room. The large bed took up the center of the space with a luxurious en suite bath. Georgia set her bag down on the foot of the bed. "Hopefully you'll be comfortable up here."

Misty looked around and slipped out of her sweater. That exposed even more scars, blended in with a swirl of tattoos that disappeared beneath her short-sleeved shirt. "They're track marks," she said, noticing Georgia looking. "Well, not all of them. Some of them are leftover from my cutting phase."

Georgia knew her mother had a heroin problem, but she hadn't heard about the cutting. "You cut yourself?"

She nodded. "Yes. That was from my younger years. I was a messed-up kid. Cutting myself made me feel better. It was my only release. At least until I found drugs and sex." She shook her head and ran her palms over her bare arms. "I should've stuck with the cutting. I didn't hurt anyone but myself."

Georgia couldn't help giving her mother another hug. She was the parent, the one who should be comforting her daughter, but in reality, Misty was just a lost child. Georgia wasn't sure she wanted to know about what set her down this path of self-destruction, but she knew she wanted to help her make a different life for herself.

"You're turning things around," she said. "You've got plenty of time to live a different life."

"Do you think so?" Misty asked. Her gray eyes, exactly like Georgia's, were red and brimming with tears.

"I know so."

Nine

"The results are back."

Carson had opened the front door of his loft expecting to see Georgia, but instead he found Graham and Brooks standing there. Graham was holding a large envelope. All thoughts of his dinner plans with her evaporated when he realized what it was. He had been awaiting and dreading this moment all week.

"Have you looked at the results yet?"

"No," Graham said. "I practiced an amazing amount of restraint because I thought it was best that we all look at it together."

"With alcohol," Brooks added, holding up an expensive bottle of tequila in one hand and a bag of limes in the other.

"That's probably wise," Carson noted.

Stepping back, he let his brothers in. He expected them to want to rush to the results, considering how hard they'd worked to uncover the truth and how long they'd waited. But they took their time. Graham poured shots while Brooks sliced up a few limes. Carson just watched anxiously, tapping his fingers on the quartz countertops while he waited.

There was something final about reading the lab report, like the end of an era. For their whole lives, their father had been a mystery to them. Carson was certain that each of them had entertained private fantasies about what their father was really like and what he would say to them if they ever came face-to-face. It was possible that this envelope could shatter those fantasies once and for all. If the test results came back positive, the mystery was over and they were left with the cold, hard reality of Sutton Winchester being their father.

If the results were negative, they had to start back at square one. This time with no leads to follow. The only evidence they'd found pointed to Sutton. If he wasn't the answer, Carson was at a loss for where to look next.

As he looked down at the envelope, their mother's words echoed through his mind. *You're better off without your father in your life,* she'd said. What if she was right? This was their last chance to change their minds.

"Are you guys sure you want to do this?" Carson asked.

"Are you serious?" Graham asked.

"Yes, I'm serious." Carson picked up the envelope and held it up. "Once we open this thing, there's no going back. Mom kept our father out of our lives for a reason. Maybe it was the right decision."

"Maybe, but we've come too far to turn back now," Brooks argued. "Besides, Sutton will have the results, too. It's too late to change our minds. We're going to find out one way or another."

"You're right," Carson admitted and tossed the envelope back onto the counter. And it was true. They were past the point of no return.

Graham handed a shot out to each of them. "Let's do one to take the edge off before we open the results. What shall we drink to?"

"The truth," Carson offered. Good or bad, at least they'd finally have that.

"The truth," his brothers repeated in unison. Together they all drank their shots of smooth tequila, not even needing the limes when they were through. They sat their shot glasses down and one by one, their gazes returned to the unopened envelope.

"Hurry up and open it," Brooks said at last. "The suspense is killing me."

"Who wants to read it aloud?" Graham asked as he slid his finger beneath the seal and opened the envelope.

"You do it," Carson said. "You're the one who made this happen."

Graham pulled out two sheets of paper, one with Carson's results and one with the twins' results. "Okay. Let's start with Carson." His gaze danced back and forth across the paper for a moment, making Carson's stomach tangle into knots as he waited. Not even the tequila could tame it.

"The alleged father, Sutton Winchester, *cannot* be excluded as the biological father of the child, Carson Newport, since they share genetic markers. Using the above systems, the probability of paternity is 99.99%, as compared to an untested, unrelated man of the Caucasian population."

"We were right," Brooks said.

Carson didn't know how to react to the news. He'd braced himself for this moment, part of him hoping Sutton wasn't his father and part of him hoping he was, just so he'd have the answer at last. Well, now he had it. He was that old bastard's son. He'd known in his heart that he was, but having the official confirmation just sealed it in his mind.

The man he'd been looking for his whole life, the one his mother warned him about, had been right under his nose the whole time. Sutton had always treated him like a nuisance. The Newport Corporation and its owners were just an annoying fly buzzing around the King of Chicago's crown. He'd never once treated them like anything else, certainly not like his own children. It was one thing not to be able to publicly acknowledge your illegitimate sons, but to deliberately handle them like pebbles in his shoe their whole lives…

"Carson, are you okay?" Brooks asked.

He realized that he'd been holding his breath and let it out in one big burst. "Yes." He reached for the tequila bottle and did another shot without them. "Let's read yours and get this over with."

Graham shuffled the papers in his hands until he could read the second report. "The alleged father, Sutton Winchester, cannot be excluded *or* confirmed as the biological father of the children, Graham and Brooks Newport. The children's samples were tainted or mishandled, containing foreign contaminants, and must be recollected and retested for final results."

"Mishandled?" Brooks exclaimed. "Are you kidding me? After all this?" Now it was his turn to reach for the bottle and take a shot.

Graham just shook his head. "I guess we need to go back tomorrow and get swabbed again."

"And while we wait for those results, we can plan how we want to move forward," Carson said, trying to distract his brothers from their disappointment. "We know at the very least that I'm his son, so we can do some contingency planning."

"No," Brooks says. "We can't wait. We need to jump on these results, especially if he's as sick as

Georgia makes him sound. Sutton has gone long enough without receiving his comeuppance. He needs to pay for abandoning us. He needs to pay for using and tossing our mother aside. He may be our father, but this is war. It's best to attack while the opposing side isn't expecting it."

Graham gave a curt nod in agreement, making Carson's stomach start to ache again. "Let's set up a meeting with the Winchesters for tomorrow."

Georgia was surprised to brush past the Newport twins as they got off the elevator in Carson's building and she was getting on. They gave her a polite wave but didn't stop to say hello. They both had a cold, calculating look in their eyes that worried her. What had happened? She got the feeling her date with Carson would be different from what they'd planned.

She waited patiently after ringing the doorbell. When Carson finally answered, the expression on his face worried her even more than his brothers' scheming scowls. He looked heartbroken. His mouth was drawn down into an uncharacteristic frown and his face was flushed. His eyes looked a little red and his brow was furrowed in thought.

"Hey, Georgia," he said in a flat tone. "I have to apologize in advance. I'm not going to be very good company tonight. Do you mind if we don't go out?"

"We can stay in," Georgia said and pushed past him into his apartment. She got the feeling he wanted to turn her away, and she wouldn't let him. He needed someone to talk to, and she was going to be the one whether he liked it or not.

She set her purse down on the counter beside a half-empty bottle of tequila and three shot glasses. That explained the flushed face and red eyes. Then her gaze ran across the paperwork and the lab logo across the top. He'd gotten the results of the paternity test.

Georgia didn't need to read the papers. She could tell by the look on Carson's face that Sutton was the father he'd never wanted. Turning to face him, she wrapped her arms around his waist and looked up into his green eyes. "Are you going to be okay?"

"Eventually. I just have to forget about everything I know to be true and adjust to a world where a man like Sutton could produce a man like me."

"Sutton didn't produce a man like you, Carson. If he had been in your life, you'd be a completely different person and likely one I wouldn't date. He might be your genetic contributor, but you were produced by the loving environment your mother raised you in. That's what's important. You're nothing like him."

"Oh really?" He pulled away and wandered into the living room, where he dropped down onto the couch. "I'm more of a cutthroat bastard than you might think. We're going to destroy him, you know."

Georgia's eyes widened. "What do you mean?"

"Graham and Brooks want to go after his estate.

ANDREA LAURENCE

No holds barred. They think we're owed something after years of neglect and now is their chance to make Sutton pay the piper."

Georgia sat down on the couch beside him and rested her hand on his knee. "You don't agree with their plans?"

"I do and I don't. I mean, I want him to suffer. I want him to spend the rest of his life regretting what he did to my mother and to us. But at the same time, I guess I just don't have the killer instinct. That's the one thing I wish I had inherited from him."

"Don't wish that. It's your conscientiousness that I'm drawn to."

Carson looked at her with some of his previous sparkle in his eyes. "You mean it's not my dashing good looks and rock-hard abs?"

Georgia smiled wide. She was happy to see a glimmer of her Carson beneath the gloom. "Those certainly don't hurt."

He wrapped his arm around her shoulders, and Georgia snuggled in against his chest. "I'm glad you came over tonight. If I was alone, I'd probably stew all evening and finish off that bottle of tequila."

"You'd regret it tomorrow."

"I usually do. But enough of my parental drama. I don't want to waste our night together talking about that. But I do have to ask how it's going with your mom. Hopefully better news than on my end."

"Good. Better than I ever could've expected or

hoped," Georgia said. She knew that Carson was feeling down, but she was filled with more optimism than she'd felt in years. Maybe even her whole life. The last few days had been amazing. She'd gotten answers to questions she'd never even thought to ask. "We've spent hours talking. I've learned so much about her and my family that I've never met. Did you know I have a brother and sister somewhere?"

"Really?" He chuckled and slowly shook his head. "That seems to be going around lately. I've suddenly got more siblings than I know what to do with."

"The hardest part, though, is hearing about her life. I mean, I thought I had it rough growing up in the foster care system, but it's nothing compared to what she went through. I'm not surprised she turned to drugs. I don't even know how she gets out of bed every morning."

"Where is she now? We could've rescheduled tonight until after she went back to Michigan."

"No, that's okay. It actually worked out perfectly. I helped her find a local Alcoholics Anonymous support group that meets tonight. It's just a few blocks from my place in a church, so I gave her enough money to get herself some authentic Chicago-style deep-dish pizza from a place across the street from it. That will keep her busy for a few hours."

"Are you okay leaving her alone in your apartment?"

This again. "She's been alone all day while I've

been at the office and there hasn't been a problem. I appreciate your concern, Carson, but I think it will be okay. If I was worried, I wouldn't be here with you."

"Okay. You can smack me for being overcautious. I know I'm being selfish, but I'd much rather you be here with me, anyway. I just wish I was better company." Carson gave her a weak smile. "I figured I wouldn't get to see you after work hours until Misty had left."

Georgia didn't want to wait that long to spend time with Carson. At the office, it just wasn't the same. They kept things distant and professional, the way they should have. Their conversations were about business—planning the charity gala for the hospital was the big task of the moment. She didn't get to snuggle against his chest and feel his arms around her the way she wanted them to be.

"Well, I miss you," she said. Georgia didn't like the way it felt to admit vulnerability like that, but it was true. Whether or not this fling of theirs lasted through the month, she'd found herself getting increasingly attached to Carson. She wanted to tell him about how things were going with her mom. She wanted to be there to soothe him when he got bad news. "And I'm glad I came over. I wouldn't want you to be home alone tonight."

"You make me not want to be home alone any night."

Leaning into her, he pressed his lips against hers. The soft touch rapidly intensified as the taste of tequila and emotion mixed together on her tongue. She drank in his sadness, doing whatever she could to make him feel better tonight. She would use her body like a bandage to cover the wounds his father left without ever realizing it.

Pulling away from Carson's mouth, she smiled coyly at him. "I know what will make you feel better."

He lifted a curious eyebrow but didn't question her. Instead he waited for her to reveal her answer. Without speaking, she slipped off the couch onto the floor in front of him. On her knees, she eased between his legs. Her gaze stayed fixed on his as she slowly unbuttoned his shirt.

Carson didn't argue. He just took a deep breath and let her do as she pleased. Georgia tugged the shirt out of his waistband, unbuttoning the last of the buttons and opening it to expose his chest. Leaning in, she planted a line of kisses starting at his collarbone and moving down. She noticed how the hair on his belly thickened as she traveled lower, planting one last kiss above his belt and drawing in the warm scent of his skin before she sat back to unbuckle it. Her fingers moved deftly to unbutton his pants and zip his fly open. She could feel the heat of his desire pressing against her hand through the cotton of his underwear.

Georgia let her palm glide over it ever so slowly before she gathered the waistbands and tugged both his pants and underwear down his thighs. With nothing left in her way, she curled her fingers around the length of him and gave a little squeeze until he hissed and squirmed on the sofa. She let her hot breath blow across his skin before she bent her head and took him into her mouth.

Her tongue glided along his smooth skin as her lips pressed farther and farther down. Carson's whole body tensed the lower she moved. He didn't even breathe until she eased back.

"Oh, Georgia," he groaned, threading his fingers through her blond waves and holding tight. His grip didn't hurt, but the intensity urged her on. "Damn, you feel good, baby."

She worked into a slow, tortuous rhythm between her mouth and her hands. Carson's fingertips massaged her scalp, never forcing her movements, but going along with them. She could feel every muscle in his body tighten as she sped up, then slowed down to tease him.

"I don't think I can take much more of this," he managed through gritted teeth.

"I'm just getting started."

"Yeah, well, so am I. Come here," he said. Reaching out, he took her hand and tugged her up until she was straddling him. He took a moment to slip on a condom, and then pushed the hem of her pencil skirt up to her hips, brushing over the lace tops of her thigh-high hosiery. His hands slipped beneath her legs, feeling at the insignificant scrap of fabric that separated them. His fingers pushed the lace aside, allowing the length of him to seek out her opening.

Georgia took it from there. She slowly lowered her hips, taking in every inch of him until she was fully seated on his lap. He reached for her blouse, unbuttoning the silk fabric and slipping it off her shoulders to the floor. His palms covered the cream lace bra, molding the full globes of her breasts in his hands and pinching at the hardened nipples that strained against the rough material.

Closing her eyes, Georgia rolled her hips, moving him inside her. A low growl sounded from Carson's throat as she eased up and slid down the length of him again. She bit her bottom lip as the movements started to generate a liquid heat in her belly.

"Why did I wait so long to touch you?" Carson wondered aloud. "You could've been in my arms all this time."

The same thought had crossed Georgia's mind in the last week. She'd been at the Newport Corporation for over a year now. A year when she'd gone home each night fantasizing about her boss and never believing she could have him. A year of loneliness that could've been spent with him if she had thought for a moment that she deserved a man like him.

She still wasn't entirely sure she was good enough,

but she'd savor every moment she could share with him. Georgia had never let herself get truly close to someone, but she felt Carson getting past all her barriers. He was the first man even to try, and the stone walls just tumbled at his slightest touch. Her heart swelled at the thought of him, and her body craved him.

She wasn't entirely sure she knew what love felt like. She'd read about it in books and seen examples in movies, but she'd never felt it herself. But now, here with Carson, she thought she might finally know for sure. It was more than like, more than just need or desire. He consumed her, body and soul, and she never wanted to let him go.

Georgia was falling in love with him.

The rush of emotions spilled from her heart, and the pleasurable coil inside her grew that much tighter. As the sensations grew more intense, Carson shifted his hands to grip her hips. His fingertips pressed into her flesh. Her thighs started to burn as she moved faster, coaxing the release from deep inside her. Soft cries and whimpers of anticipation escaped her lips as her climax grew nearer and nearer.

"Yeah," Carson whispered in soft encouragement. "Let go, Georgia."

She didn't have any choice in the matter. Her orgasm exploded inside her, the shockwaves radiating through her whole body. He steadied her hips and she braced herself against his shoulders as she writhed and cried out. Her muscles clamped down around him, fluttering and pulsing as the final throbs of pleasure echoed and then finally faded away. When she opened her eyes, she found Carson watching her.

"You are so beautiful," he said. "And you're even more amazing when you come undone. I love to watch you let go and just feel."

Georgia felt a blush rise to her cheeks. "Well, now it's your turn," she said, clamping her inner muscles down hard around him.

He groaned as his hands slid up from her hips until they were wrapped around her back. He pulled her torso toward him until she was hunched over him with her face buried in his neck. Keeping a tight grip on her, he started moving beneath her.

Georgia gasped and clung to him as her overstimulated nerves tried to absorb more pleasure. Her lips danced across the salty skin of his neck and shoulder, tasting and nipping at him. As he tensed and his moves became more frantic, she whispered a few provocative and erotic things into his ear.

It wasn't what she wanted to say. In the moment, overflowing with emotions and sensations, she wanted to whisper that she was falling in love with him, but it wasn't the right time or place. She'd never said the words before, and when she did, she wanted it to be special. She wanted him to respond in kind. That, she feared, would take more time.

What she *did* say was just right, however. Carson's fingers dug into her flesh as he thrust hard and poured into her with a satisfied roar. Georgia rode through the waves, planting a soft kiss on his lips once he stilled beneath her.

"You know what?" he said when he caught his breath.

"What?"

"You were right. I do feel better."

Ten

Carson had trouble sleeping that night after Georgia went home. He didn't know if it was his ever-evolving feelings for her or his nerves about his meeting at Elite Industries the next day, but by the time he and his brothers arrived at Sutton's offices that afternoon, he felt very unprepared.

"This isn't the way to Sutton's office," Graham said as the assistant took the three brothers down the hallway.

"Yes, sir. This is the way to Miss Winchester's office. Mr. Winchester isn't in today."

"That bastard stood us up," Brooks grumbled. "He got the results the same as we did and he was too big a coward to show his face."

"Actually," Eve Winchester said from just ahead of them, "he's quite ill."

Carson narrowed his gaze at Eve, Sutton's oldest daughter. Based on what Tammy had said, Eve was already born when his parents split up, so that meant Eve was his older sister. It was hard enough to think about Sutton as his father, but the shockwaves that radiated through the family were equally difficult. His sister. He ran his fingers through his hair and shook his head. He wasn't going to adjust to this easily.

"I'm sure he is feeling poorly," Brooks said, "after being caught in such a big lie."

Eve's thin frame tensed at Brooks's words. Instead of responding, she waved them past her into her office to sit at the conference room table.

Looking down the table, Carson noticed Brooks was wound tight and ready to fight. Graham was uncharacteristically silent, but his eyes never left Eve. She sat down across from them. A moment later, another woman arrived. She was tinier than Eve with lighter blond hair. They both had the same green eyes, though. Sutton's eyes. Carson's eyes.

"This is my youngest sister, Grace."

"Where's Nora?" Brooks asked. "I believe we requested to meet with everyone today."

"Nora lives in Colorado and has a small child. Since you demanded this meeting take place today, you'll understand that it was impossible for her to make it."

"And Sutton?" Graham said at last. "Is he really sick or just sick at the thought of more of his money being funneled away?"

Carson watched the Winchester women as they reacted to Graham's cutting words. He could see the worry in Grace's eyes. He knew then that Sutton truly was ill. "What's wrong with him?" he asked. He was his father, after all.

"We don't know," Grace replied. "He's seeing the doctor today."

"Let's cut to the chase, gentlemen." Eve stared all of them down, her cold, businesslike demeanor reminding Carson very much of their father. "I can run this business and this family just as well as my father, so I see no reason why we can't proceed without him."

"Well," Carson began, "we presume that your father received the results of the paternity tests and has informed you of what they revealed."

"He did. You are our half brother," Eve said matter-of-factly. Turning to the twins, she added, "You two are to be determined."

"I'm pretty sure the results will turn out positive this time," Brooks said. "So we wanted to get the process started."

"The process of what?" Grace asked.

"The process of ensuring that we get our share of the Winchester estate."

"Our father is sick, not dead. There's no estate to have yet."

"There will be one day. He won't live forever, even with all his money. We're not about to wait until he's six feet under to start contesting the will. We intend to make sure we get what's coming to us, fair and square."

Carson sat uncomfortably as his brothers and sisters argued back and forth.

"And how do you propose this miracle will happen?" Eve asked. "It doesn't matter if you're biologically Winchesters or not. Our father doesn't have to include anyone in his will he doesn't want to."

"That's true," Graham said. "He can leave us out. But if he does, I can guarantee that you and your sisters will never see a penny of your inheritances. We will sue and tie the estate up in court for years. You won't get a thing until it's settled by the judge, and by then, half of it might have been drained away in legal fees."

Grace swallowed hard. "And what is our alternative?"

"It's fairly simple," Brooks said. "If your father voluntarily updates his will now, we'll have no problem. We've already gone our entire lives being ignored. Our mother raised us alone without receiving a dime in child support from our father. I don't think it's too much to ask that we get our share once he's gone. We think you ladies can help make that happen."

"Us?" Eve asked.

"You're daddy's little girls, right? Encourage your father to update the will to include us with even distribution among all the biological children. Tell him that you don't want to fight family in court over the estate. Certainly he'll listen to you."

"Have you met our father?" Eve asked.

At that, Carson had to chuckle. All four of his siblings looked over at him with venom in their expressions. Now was not the time to find amusement in the situation. He opted to try diffusing the tension instead.

"Eve, Grace," he said, "try to see this from our point of view. You had your father in your life. You had everything you've ever wanted. We were equally deserving, but we were shut out. We had to fight for everything we have, and we're not going to stop now. Our father owes us this, for our mother's sake and for the sake of the children he abandoned."

"I am very sorry for the way you all grew up. I'm sorry that you felt unloved and had a difficult life. But you do understand that this has nothing to do with us girls? Have you given any consideration to how we feel about all of this?" Eve looked at Carson as she said the words, making him feel like the bully in the situation. "We suddenly have brothers?

Or, at least, one for certain. We are faced with the knowledge that our father not only cheated on our mother but also did it in such a reckless way. You're not punishing Sutton with this proposal of yours. You're punishing us."

"I hate that's the way it has to be," Graham said, with a touch of sadness in his voice that Carson didn't expect. He was used to Graham being a shark in this kind of negotiation. Perhaps he wasn't as enthusiastic about using his sharp teeth on his own sister.

"But you and I both know that there's only one way to get to Sutton Winchester," Graham continued, "and that's through his wallet. We're not going to get a tearful reunion out of him. Hell, we'll be lucky to get him to acknowledge us privately, much less publicly. I'm sorry that we have to rob your trust funds to make it happen, but money is all we're going to get out of our father, so you'd better be damn sure that we're going to get it."

The room was awkwardly silent for a moment as all the potential siblings sized one another up. "Very well," Eve said at last. "I'll have a discussion with Father about the will. When the new DNA test results are ready, perhaps he will be willing to move forward with updates. But not until then."

"Fair enough," Graham answered.

"Well, then, if there's nothing else, I'm sure we all have businesses to run." Eve pushed up from her chair, and everyone else followed suit.

"We'll see ourselves out," Carson said as they spilled out into the hallway. He was certain the sisters had plenty of talking to do among themselves. As did the brothers.

They moved silently through the offices until they climbed into Brooks's car and slammed the doors shut.

"Now what?" Carson asked.

"I think that went well," Graham said. "I think we wait on the results and see what they do next."

"You were too soft on them," Brooks complained to Graham. "That Eve woman is just your type. She had you eating from her hand."

"That Eve woman might be our sister, man. That's gross."

"Well, either way, she's your type and you didn't go in for the kill."

"There wasn't need to. We got our point across. Like she said, they're being punished for their father's actions. I'm not going to push harder until we have to."

Carson listened to the twins argue. He wasn't sure how he felt about their plans to get revenge against Sutton. "I don't know about all this," he said.

Both brothers turned toward the backseat to look at him. "What do you mean?" Brooks asked.

"I mean…what's the point? We don't need the money. We're not going to get a dad out of this. We're just going to make our sisters hate us, and when Sutton is gone, they might be all we have left."

"He dumped our mother, Carson. He left her pregnant with infant twins to care for. He needs to be punished. Tell me another way to do it and I'll do it," Graham offered.

There wasn't another way and he knew it. "I don't know."

Brooks's expression softened as he looked at Carson. "This isn't the kind of thing Mom raised us to do, I know, but her memory demands vengeance. If you don't want our mother's blood money, funnel it into the hospital. Buy equipment that will save children's lives, if that's what helps you sleep at night. But it's happening and you need to get used to the idea. We're going to get our pound of flesh from Winchester."

Georgia was surprised by a voice mail from Sutton at the office when she returned from lunch. She thought that he was meeting with the Newport brothers today, but the message indicated he was calling her from home. He wanted to speak with her and give her his donation check personally. If she was available, he would send a car to pick her up.

She had no idea where the Winchester home was, but she was pretty sure the "L" didn't go there, so she made arrangements with his secretary to be picked up within the hour.

She knew she'd made a promise to Carson that she would tell him when she went to see Sutton, but it would have to wait until tomorrow. He would be tied up with his brothers and their scheming, she had no doubt, and tonight she was spending time with her mother. She was leaving in the morning for Detroit, and Georgia was planning to make a special dinner.

It took quite a while to get out to Sutton's estate, but when she arrived, she was stunned by the extravagance of it all. Large iron gates protected the winding driveway that led to the giant gray mansion. It sprawled on forever, easily housing twenty people or more instead of the five Winchesters she knew about.

The driver circled the courtyard fountain and pulled up to the front steps. He opened the door and let Georgia out. An older man in a suit was waiting for her at the entrance.

"Miss Adams," he greeted her with a polite smile. "I am Christopher, the butler. Mr. Winchester is expecting you."

"I thought Mr. Winchester would be in the office today," she said.

"Normally he would be, but he's not feeling well."

Georgia followed Christopher up the marble staircase to the second floor of the mansion. They headed toward a set of double doors at the end of the hallway. "Are we going to his office?" she asked.

"No, ma'am. He's not well enough to leave his bed today. You'll be meeting with him in the master suite." Christopher pushed open the double doors and moved ahead.

She wasn't too keen on the idea of being in Sutton Winchester's bedroom, but it was too late to do anything about it. As she looked around, it hardly seemed like a bedroom anyway. It was almost like an apartment in itself with its own seating area, dressing area, a desk and a wall of French doors that led out to a private balcony overlooking the pool and tennis courts. Up ahead, another set of doors led to the bedroom itself.

Christopher opened the second set of doors. "Mr. Winchester, Miss Adams is here to see you."

"Good, send her in. And have some tea sent up."

Christopher disappeared, leaving Georgia alone in Sutton's bedroom. The minute she laid eyes on him, however, all her worries disappeared. This was not a man luring her here for seduction.

He looked even more sunken and thin than he had a few days ago. The circles under his eyes were darker. There was an IV in his hand and some medical equipment tracking his heart rate and other vital signs nearby. An oxygen tube was inserted into his nose and wrapped around his ears.

"I'm afraid I'm going to have to rescind my offer to be your lover, Georgia." He said the words with a smile, but there was no twinkle of amusement in his familiar green eyes.

She couldn't help her gaze from widening at the

sight of him propped up in his bed. "They said you were sick, but this is more than just sick, isn't it?"

"Unfortunately. Please, have a seat." Sutton gestured to a chair at his bedside.

"I thought you were meeting with the Newport boys today to talk about the test results."

"That was the plan, but this damn cancer has other ideas. Eve is handling it."

"Cancer?"

"That's what they tell me," he said with a defeated tone. "Stage IV lung cancer. They haven't tested yet, but they're pretty sure it's spread. Probably to my lymph nodes. My doctor will be trying some things, but this is basically a death sentence. Some people would say it's long overdue."

"Does your family know yet?"

Sutton shook his head. "No. The girls know I'm ill, but not to what extent. I'm going to meet with the children in a few days to tell them everything once the plans are finalized. This is a very delicate situation, Georgia, and I need you to promise to keep my illness a secret. You can't tell anyone, especially Carson. I need to tell them all this in my own way, in my own time."

Georgia could only nod. Her heart was breaking on the inside for Carson. He'd only learned about his father the day before, and now he was going to lose him before he'd even gotten to know him. It didn't seem fair that she was getting a second chance with her long-lost parent and he wouldn't have the same.

A woman arrived in the room with a silver tea service just then. She laid everything out on the nearby nightstand, pouring them both a delicate china cup of hot black tea. She quickly prepared Sutton's tea as he liked it, then handed him the cup and saucer with a buttery piece of shortbread on the edge.

"How do you take your tea, miss?" she asked.

"One sugar and a splash of cream, please."

The woman handed her a cup. "Is there anything else I can get you, Mr. Winchester?"

"No, thank you. That will be all."

The woman nodded and disappeared as quickly as she had arrived.

Georgia studied her tea, taking a tentative sip as she thought over everything Sutton had told her. "Why are you telling me before anyone else? Why did you ask me here today?" She hated being burdened with this knowledge, knowing how it would affect Carson and his brothers.

"Because I like you, Georgia. You're smart. You're attractive. You've got a great head for business. If I was twenty years younger, you would be in trouble." He sighed wistfully and shook his head. "But my mind and my body don't really cooperate the way I'd like them to anymore. I asked you here today because I wanted to tell you this in person so you'd understand where I was coming from. Since you and Carson are together, I thought maybe you could help him process it all."

Georgia was surprised by Sutton's thoughtfulness. Despite his physical and emotional distance from his son, he seemed to know that this would be hard on Carson. And not only that, but he knew, too, that Carson wouldn't turn to him for comfort—he would go to Georgia.

"I also wanted to give you something."

Sutton reached over to his nightstand and pulled out a sealed envelope from the top drawer. It had Carson's name written on the front in his handwriting. "This is the check I promised you for the hospital. I wanted to give it to you personally. Please see to it that Carson gets this when you see him next."

Georgia took the envelope from him and slipped it into her purse. "I will."

"He hates me, you know?" Sutton said matter-of-factly. "I've given him every reason to. I doubt that check will help, but it's all I can offer. Cindy was a bright spot in my life. When I lost her, I gave in to the darkness once and for all. Honoring her memory by contributing to the children's hospital is the least I can do."

Georgia couldn't help but notice the soft, sentimental expression on Sutton's face when he talked about Carson's mother and how he referred to her as Cindy. Was there more between them than just one more of his dalliances? She and Carson would probably never know. But she did understand how Carson felt.

"He doesn't hate you," Georgia argued. "He hates how you treated his mother."

At that, Sutton laughed. "I bet Cindy told the boys quite the tale to keep them away from me. She probably did it to protect me. That's why she left the company," he said. "My wife at the time was threatening all sorts of chaos if I didn't break it off with Cindy. I couldn't do it, though. I didn't care if she ruined me. But Cindy cared. She said she wouldn't let me give up everything for her, and she left. All I could do was give her a severance package to ease the loss. She told me not to look for her. She made me promise, so I kept my word. I wish every day that I hadn't. I would've known about Carson if I'd searched for her."

Georgia perked up in her seat. "You didn't know about Carson?"

Sutton shook his head. "No. I knew about the twins, of course, but they weren't mine. When they started their business and became my main competitors, I knew who they were. I started to contact Cindy, then thought better of it. It had been a long time and she probably didn't want me interrupting her life. When I realized there was a younger Newport boy, I figured he was the child of Cindy's next lover. It never occurred to me…"

There was a sadness in Sutton's eyes that she didn't

expect to see there. "I'd always wanted a son. I love my girls more than anything, but it pains me greatly to know that I had a child out there all these years and I didn't know it. And now—" he gestured toward the medical equipment next to the bed "—it's too late."

This was a side of Sutton that Georgia had never expected to see. He wasn't a saint by any stretch of the imagination, but he wasn't the monster he'd been painted to be, either. She felt a genuine pain coming from him as he spoke about his regrets. Perhaps she was right and his relationship with Carson's mother had been more than just a sleazy affair. It sounded like love to her. She knew how that felt, and how much she was willing to do for Carson because she cared. Was Cynthia willing to go to such great lengths to protect Sutton from financial and corporate ruin?

"It's not too late," Georgia said. "You and Carson can still have a relationship. You just have to convince him to give you a chance. If all those things his mother told him about you aren't true, he needs to know that."

Sutton listened to her thoughtfully, then shook his head. "He won't listen to me. Maybe he'll listen to you."

Eleven

"Mom?"

Georgia pushed her way through the front door of her loft, her arms filled with groceries. It was late enough when she'd left the Winchester estate that she'd had the car drop her at her neighborhood grocery store instead of returning to the office. She'd picked up a few things her mother liked, and got what she needed to make her famous lasagna for dinner. Misty had been asleep when she got home from Carson's the night before, so Georgia had planned a nice evening for them to spend together before her mother took the bus back to Detroit.

She'd been feeling quite sentimental since she left Sutton. If there was hope for his relationship with

Carson, perhaps there was hope for her relationship
with Misty. Things had gone well so far.

She dropped the bags onto the dining room table
and listened for sounds of Misty in the house. The
last few days, she'd returned home to find her curled
up on the couch reading one of her books or watching television. But there was no murmur of voices
coming from the TV set or the radio.

"Mom?" she said again, but there was no answer.

Frowning, Georgia made her way through the living room. Everything seemed to be in place. The
book her mother had been reading was sitting on
the coffee table where she'd left it. The lamp was on
nearby. Perhaps she'd gone upstairs for something.

She climbed up the stairs to her bedroom loft and
stopped short when her eyes took in the sight. There
it seemed like a tornado had flown around the room.
All her drawers were open with clothes cast to the
ground, her closet door was ajar, and her jewelry armoire had its now-empty trays tossed onto the floor.

Her first reaction was to be scared and worried
for Misty. She ran into the closet, half expecting to
find her crumpled, beaten body there. Nothing. Then
she went into the bathroom, once again hoping her
mother hadn't been attacked when her apartment
was robbed. Nothing there, either. Then she noticed
among the chaos that her mother's backpack and
duffel bag were gone.

Along with Georgia's nicer things.

She didn't have much in the way of expensive jewelry, but she had some. At least, before now she had. Everything had been cleaned out of her jewelry armoire, even the cheap costume pieces. In her closet, several pairs of expensive shoes were missing with the empty boxes left lying on the ground. Her new iPad she'd left charging on the dresser was gone, too.

There was only one thing left that was worth anything. She always kept an envelope of cash and an emergency credit card between her mattress and box springs. It was an old habit, one that would allow her to disappear at a moment's notice. With that money and the items in her purse, she could walk away and never come back. It was a remnant of her nomadic life as a foster child.

Georgia crouched down and thrust her hand beneath the mattress. She felt around, but her fingertips didn't make contact with the envelope. Finally she lifted the whole mattress up, but that just confirmed her suspicions. The money was gone. Along with her mother.

She sunk down onto the bed, her chest tight with emotions she wasn't ready to face. It had happened. Everything Carson had warned her about had happened. She'd hoped that Misty was ready to be a mother, that she'd cleaned up her act, but Georgia had been wrong. Instead Misty had gained Georgia's trust and abused it. How could she have been so naive?

Pushing herself up from the bed as the tears began

to flow, she rushed into the bathroom. She turned on the cold water and splashed her flushed, heated face. The water stung as it mixed with her angry tears and dripped back into the sink.

Georgia braced her hands on the counter and hovered there. She wasn't sure what to do now. Should she call the cops on her mother? She knew she should, but a part of her couldn't do it. Even though she was heartbroken. Even though she felt like an abandoned child sitting in an unfamiliar foster home again.

She'd come to like her mother over the past few days, and even this hadn't erased those memories. Somehow she couldn't turn her mother in to the police. The things she'd taken might've been a lot to Misty, but they weren't important to Georgia. They were all replaceable. Unlike their relationship. If they even had one.

As she stood up, her gaze fell on the nearby wastebasket. A small clear baggie with residue and a used hypodermic needle were in there among the tissue. Her mother was using again. That explained the sudden change. Had she taken the pizza money and decided to get high instead of going to AA? When she'd come home last night, was her mother passed out instead of sleeping? Probably so. Misty had let her addiction get the best of her and ruined what they'd started to build together.

Georgia was so disappointed. In her mother. In

herself. She needed to talk to someone. Going back downstairs, she picked up her phone from where she'd left it on the dining room table. She quickly dialed Carson.

"Hey, Georgia," he answered. "I wasn't expecting to hear from you tonight."

"Can I come over?" The minute she opened her mouth to speak, the tears threatened again. She fought to keep them from her voice. If she was going to break down again, it would be in his arms, and not before.

"Uh, sure. I'll warn you that I'm not very good company, but you're welcome to come by. I thought you were with your mom tonight."

Georgia swallowed the lump that had lodged in her throat. "Change of plans."

"I'll be here. See you soon."

She hung up the phone and set it back on the table. She conscientiously put all the perishable groceries away, leaving the pantry goods in the bag. Then she armed her home security system in case her mother returned for more, and headed to Carson's place. Tonight she couldn't face the "L," so she hailed a cab instead.

"Come on in, Georgia," he called as she knocked on the door. She slipped inside and closed the door behind her. "I'm in the exercise room!" he said just as she wondered where he was.

Georgia hadn't known he had an exercise room,

but she followed the sound of his voice down the hallway. There she found him in nothing but a pair of shorts and some boxing gloves. He was covered in sweat and wailing angrily on a punching bag hung from the ceiling.

She watched him for a few minutes. She kept expecting him to stop since she was here. To ask what was wrong. To console her. But he kept punching until exhaustion took over and his forehead dropped against the bag.

"Are you okay?" she asked.

"We were supposed to meet with Sutton and his daughters today," he explained as he ripped the Velcro open to pull off his gloves. "He stood us up."

She knew that wasn't entirely true, but she couldn't tell him that. She had to pretend that she didn't know. "Sutton wasn't there?"

"No," he said, throwing the gloves into the corner. "They said he was sick, which just confirms what you told me. But how sick could he be? He met with you the other day hoping for a piece of tail, but when he's supposed to meet with his own sons, he can't do it?"

Sutton had deteriorated pretty quickly. He was sicker than anyone could've guessed. "I'm not surprised. I told you he looked terrible."

"Don't defend him," Carson snapped.

Georgia flinched at his sharp criticism. Carson was completely spun up. She'd never seen him like this before. He was always fairly calm and collected, but the news about Sutton really seemed to have rattled him. "Did you meet with Eve?"

He nodded. "Eve and Grace. They weren't very receptive to our plan, but I didn't expect them to be. They weren't very receptive to me being their brother, either, as though I'd wrecked their parents' marriage by existing. Like I had anything to do with it! I just… I think this whole thing is going to blow up in our faces. Mom was right. We were better off without having our father in our lives. He was a bastard then and he's a bastard now. Nothing has changed on that front."

Georgia didn't have much to add on that note. She could tell that beneath all the blustering, he was really disappointed. The little boy deep inside had hoped his father and sisters would welcome him, just as she'd hoped her mother would be there for her. For all the good it did them. "You should give Sutton a chance to be your father. Maybe you'll be surprised by how it turns out."

Carson snatched a towel off the folded stack nearby and rubbed his face with it. "I sincerely doubt that. The man can't be trusted. I don't want you meeting with him anymore," he said.

"What? Why? I thought you wanted me to continue getting information for you."

"No. It isn't worth it. I don't want you anywhere near him. I don't want to be anywhere near him, either. I just can't believe this." Carson dropped down onto the weight bench and shook his head. "I never should've dug through my mother's things. I was better off not knowing the truth."

"You can't go back and change the past. All you can do is make the most of what's done."

Carson made an annoyed *hrmph* sound and slung the towel around his neck as he stood up. "If you don't mind, I'd rather not talk about this anymore. It will ruin the whole evening." He walked up to Georgia and gave her a kiss as he wrapped his arms around her waist. "What's going on with you? You said you were going to be with your mom tonight."

Georgia's gaze dropped to his bare chest as she nodded. "Yeah, that was the plan. But when I got home from work, I found that my mom is gone."

Carson's brow furrowed into a frown. "You mean she left early?"

"You could say that. You could also say that while I was at work, she robbed me to buy drugs and ran off."

Carson eased back so he could look her in the eye. Certainly he hadn't heard her right. "What?"

Georgia just shook her head as he pulled her tightly into his arms. "You were right all along," she said as she started to sob against his bare skin. "I thought she really wanted to be a part of my life, but she was just using me. I feel so stupid for fall-ing for this."

Carson stroked her hair as he held her close. "I'm sorry, Georgia. I didn't want to be right. I'd hoped I was wrong. Are you sure that she wasn't just out somewhere? Maybe she went to another AA meet-ing?"

"Yes, I'm sure. There was no need for her to take my iPad, emergency cash and all my jewelry for an AA meeting. She destroyed my bedroom looking for stuff she could sell. She's not coming back. And if she did, I'd turn her away."

All Carson could do was hold her. He couldn't make her mother a better person or erase what she'd done to her daughter. He could only be here for her now.

Georgia finally pulled away, rubbing the tears away from her cheeks and creating black streaks of mascara across her pale skin. "I'm sorry to just fall apart like that. Excuse me for a minute. I've cried all my mascara off. I'm going to run to the restroom and clean up a bit."

Carson nodded. "Okay. How about I pour us some wine and order a pizza? I think we both need a little alcohol and cheese tonight."

"That sounds great. Thanks."

He watched her disappear down the hallway to the powder room. Then he went to the kitchen to open some wine and dig out the pizza-delivery flyer.

Georgia's giant purse was sitting on the stack of papers he needed to search through. Since the day she'd interviewed, he'd been curious about what she had in that thing. His life fit in a wallet. What could she possibly need to carry around with her all the time?

When he lifted the straps to move the bag aside, curiosity got the best of him, and he leaned forward to peek at what she kept in there. It was hard to make out much, but he did see a white envelope with his name written on it. He knew he shouldn't do it, but he reached inside and pulled it out. When he opened the envelope, he found a check inside from Sutton. For twenty million dollars. It was made out to the Cynthia Newport Memorial Hospital for Children fund. Carson almost couldn't believe what he was looking at.

"What kind of pizz—?" Georgia stopped when she saw what was in his hand. "Did you snoop in my bag?"

"I picked it up to move it and saw this envelope with my name on it. What the hell is this about?"

"It's a check for the hospital," she said, snatching her purse from his hands. "I told you that Sutton was going to make a donation."

Carson scanned the check again and shook his head. Why had he given so much? And how long had she been holding on to it? "When did Sutton give you this check?"

Georgia frowned and her gaze dropped from his to the check in his hands. "This afternoon."

"Wait…you saw Sutton today? After he stood us all up for our meeting?"

She nodded. "He asked me to come out to his home to pick it up."

"And you didn't think to mention that to me before? You were supposed to tell me when you were going to see him. Going to his house isn't very safe, Georgia."

"You weren't around to tell. Anyway, I was going to give you that as soon as I saw you next, but I completely forgot about it with everything that happened with my mother. So here you go. He asked me to give that to you."

He wouldn't even meet his own son face-to-face, but he'd asked Georgia to come all the way out to his mansion just to give her a check? Something didn't seem right with any of this. "What did you guys talk about?"

"You, mostly."

Carson chuckled bitterly. "So he'd rather talk about me with you than actually see me or spend time with me now that he knows I'm his son?"

Georgia looked genuinely pained by his words. "You know, I don't think he's the villain you've made him out to be. All you know about him is what your mother told you and what you've learned from your cutthroat business dealings. I really think you need to spend time with him and form your own opinion."

"Why?"

"Because he's your father, Carson. You should at least give him a chance to be one to you."

"Yes, because that plan worked out so well for you and your mother." Carson snapped. It was a low blow, but he didn't care. She didn't understand what she was asking of him.

"I don't regret it, though. Yes, it didn't turn out the way I'd hoped, but at least I tried. I learned more about my past and my family—things I never would've known if I hadn't taken the chance. Yes, it cost me some personal belongings and some emotional pain, but it was worth it. You won't even give Sutton the chance."

After everything that had happened with her mother, and after Georgia had been at his side through all the drama with Sutton, Carson couldn't fathom why she would encourage him to spend time with his father. "I don't understand why you're pushing so hard for this. Whose side are you on, anyway?"

"I'm on your side, of course. Your situation with Sutton is different from mine with my mother. You've got a better shot at making this work. I would just hate for you to miss the opportunity to have a relationship with your father. That's what you've always wanted, right? You've lost so much time already. Every moment you can have with him is precious."

Sutton had said something to her. He'd woven some sob story to lure her over to his side, because she'd never stood up for him like this before. Did twenty million buy her loyalties? "What did he say to you today? What's changed?"

Georgia looked at him with conflict lining her eyes. "I can't tell you."

"You can't or you just won't? Where do your loyalties lie, Georgia? It sounds like you're choosing Sutton over me."

She gave him an indignant frown and crossed her arms over her chest. "I am not choosing Sutton over you. I want you. I only want you. I just care for you very much, and I know how important this is."

"If you cared for me, you'd tell me what he said," Carson stated.

"I can't. I gave my word that I wouldn't tell anyone before he got to talk to everyone, including you. I'm telling you this much because I care and I don't want you to do something you'll regret later. You're going to have to trust me on this."

"Trust you? How can I trust you when you've been spending so much time with him under the guise of being a spy? When my corporate rival sends me a check for twenty million dollars with you as the only courier he trusts? Am I not right to get a little suspicious?"

Georgia's eyes widened. "Twenty million dollars?"

Was she really surprised? "What? You didn't know how much he'd written it for? Certainly he didn't give me this much out of the kindness of his heart. This had to be some kind of payment, like you've earned every penny on your back."

Georgia gasped, her mouth dropping open in surprise. "That's a hateful thing to say, Carson. My dedication to your mother's charity only goes so far. I have not, nor would I ever, have something to do with Sutton outside business."

"Why else would he give me that much? Does he have a sudden fondness for sick children?" He shook his head and put the check on the counter. "I guess I should give you a raise for going above and beyond for the company. Not everyone at the Newport Corporation has that much dedication to their job."

Georgia stumbled back as though he'd struck her. It truly felt as though he had. She reached out for the counter to stabilize herself and gather her wits. "You can take that raise and shove it, along with the job, *Mr. Newport*. I thought we really had something, but I was being naive. You've spent your whole life thinking you aren't good enough and didn't deserve a woman's love, so you wouldn't know it if it bit you. You'd rather push me away, so fine. Your wish is granted. If you can't trust me, then we don't have anything. I didn't go behind your back and I didn't

sleep with your father. I don't want to be with someone, or work for someone, who could ever think otherwise."

His brow raised in surprise. "You're quitting?"

"Yes. I think I am."

Carson crossed his arms defensively over his
chest. "Are you going to run back to Sutton and beg
for that job he offered you?"

"I'm not going to dignify that with an answer. I
knew it was a bad idea to get involved with you. I
shouldn't have let my emotions rule my head. Lesson learned."

Turning on her heel, she marched out of Carson's
apartment. Angry tears streamed down her cheeks
as she exited the building and stopped at the street
corner to wait for the light. She pulled a tissue out of
her purse and blew her nose. She was getting tired
of crying.

The day had started out so well. She'd been bask-
ing in her newly discovered love for Carson and her
budding relationship with her mother. And now, only
twelve hours later, she had nothing—including a reason to stay around Chicago. She needed a break from
this town.

Raising her arm to hail a taxi, she climbed inside
one as it stopped at the curb.

"Where to?" he asked.

"O'Hare Airport."

Georgia wanted someone who would listen to her.

She couldn't count on her mother or her lover for that. The only person she could count on, the only person she'd ever been truly able to trust, was her old social worker, Sheila. She gave the best advice in the world and maybe, just maybe, she could help Georgia sort her way out of his mess.

Twelve

Carson sat on his couch, staring at his silent cell phone. It had been three days since Georgia walked out, and there hadn't been the slightest sign of her. He didn't think she would call, not really. After everything that had happened that night, he expected her to tuck her tail and go running back to Sutton. He did, however, expect her to at least show up at work to pack up her things.

So far, her office remained dark and untouched. He could've had Rebecca pack it for her, but frankly, he was hoping she would change her mind about quitting. They had no business dating, but she was still a damn good PR person, and it would be hard to replace her. He needed to remind himself of this exact moment if he ever looked at another employee with interest again.

He was just about to set his phone back on the coffee table when it rang in his hand. It was Graham's ringtone, not Georgia's.

"Yes?" he answered.

"I have news," Graham said. "Sutton has called a meeting for tomorrow. We're all to be there, but he didn't elaborate on why."

"I suppose he'll show up for his own meeting," Carson said bitterly. As he said it, he was reminded of what Georgia had said to him—that Sutton was waiting to make some kind of announcement that she couldn't share with him. This must be it, although Carson couldn't fathom what it could be about. Bringing all the kids together seemed like a recipe for disaster. "Do you think Eve was able to talk him into changing the will?"

"I have no idea. If she did, I've underestimated her, because she's worked a miracle in days."

"Will we get the test results back before we meet with them?" The paternity test on the twins was being run a second time, and they expected to hear from the lab any day now.

"Who knows? Maybe that's what Sutton is anticipating. If he knows we're his sons and the test is just a formality, he may be tired of fighting and ready to just accept us even without the results back.

I'll let Rebecca know to put it on our calendars for tomorrow."

If Sutton was about to deliver the news that Georgia had hinted at, it would be big. Big enough that she couldn't tell him despite how many times he demanded she do it. "Okay," he replied after an extended silence.

The line was quiet for a moment. "Carson, what's wrong?"

Carson had deliberately not mentioned the blowup with Georgia to his brothers. They had enough to worry about with Sutton. They didn't need his relationship drama on top of the task of finding a new PR director to handle the hospital promotions.

"Is it Georgia?" Graham pressed. "I noticed she wasn't in the office today. She hasn't quit to go work for Sutton, has she?"

Carson couldn't avoid the topic any longer. "She has quit, but I don't know where's she's gone."

"What happened?"

"This crap with Sutton happened, and when she said some things I didn't like, I lashed out at her. Then she quit."

"Sorry, man. I guess that's why you don't date coworkers. When you break up, it impacts everything else. Should I have HR open a requisition for a new PR person?"

"Not yet," Carson said, although he really didn't know why. The odds were that Georgia was not coming back. He certainly wouldn't after what was said between them. "Give it a few days," he suggested. "Let's deal with Sutton's meeting and the fallout from that first."

One fire at a time.

"Here you go, sweetie."

Georgia looked up and took the cup of hot tea from her friend and former social worker, Sheila. "Thank you," she said. "And thank you for taking me in for a few days. I just didn't know where else to go."

Sheila took her own cup of tea with her to sit in the wingback chair beside the couch where Georgia was lounging with a blanket. She'd called from O'Hare, and when she showed up on Sheila's doorstep in Detroit at nearly midnight without so much as a change of clothes, she was welcomed like family.

She supposed that was what Sheila was to her. The only family she'd ever had. She'd been there for her since she was assigned her case when Georgia was ten. Sheila did her best to place Georgia in the most stable, safe homes she could, but there weren't always a lot of options, so she tried to help in other ways. She assisted Georgia with her college and scholarship applications. She encouraged her to go to Northwestern and make something of herself. She'd also counseled her that finding her real family wasn't always the best decision.

Sheila hit the nail on the head with that advice.

"I'll help around the house while I'm here," Georgia added. As a new foster child in a home, she always found she was accepted more readily if she became useful. "I don't want you spoiling me like a houseguest."

"You've had a pretty rough week," Sheila said. "And even if you hadn't, I'd still spoil you because you deserve it. You can help if you want to, but there's really no need. I doubt two grown women will make much of a mess to worry about."

Georgia accepted her words and sipped at her tea. It was hot but not too hot, with the perfect splash of cream and sugar like the cup she'd had at Sutton's estate. How had everything in her life fallen apart since that day? She'd fallen in love, had a breakthrough with Sutton and was really getting somewhere with Misty, and the hospital project was coming along so well. Now she was single, motherless and unemployed.

"Do you have any plans while you're in Detroit?"

"Not really. I fled here before I really had a game plan. I just knew I had to get out of Chicago. But now that I'm here, I'm starting to wonder if I should go back at all."

"Why would you say that?"

"There's nothing for me there. I can unload my loft pretty easily and have my things shipped here. I don't have a job or friends there. My whole life was about my work. A fresh start in Detroit might be just what I need."

Sheila didn't bother to mask her frown. "You're talking nonsense, honey. For the work you do, Chicago is where you need to be. You love your apartment. You don't need a car like you would here. You may think there isn't much for you in Chicago, but there's certainly more than there is here. All you have in Detroit are bad memories."

"That's not true," Georgia said. "Misty said that I have a brother and sister here in Detroit that she gave up for adoption. I thought I might be able to track them down. Do you think you could help me do that?"

"That's a tricky thing to do. It depends a lot on how the adoption was done. They might not even know they were adopted if their parents didn't tell them. I'll do what I can within the limits of my job, but you might not find what you're looking for with them, either."

"What am I looking for?" Georgia asked.

"A family. You didn't get what you wanted with your mother, and I don't think it will pan out with your siblings, either. I've been doing this work for a long time, and there aren't a lot of happy endings. If I were you, instead of working so hard and focusing on the past, I'd focus on your future and having a family of your own."

A family of her own?

Honestly, that was something that had never really taken root in her mind. Her fleeting time with Carson, such as it was, was the closest thing she'd had to a serious relationship. The idea of marriage and commitment was an alien concept, and after her breakup with Carson, it seemed to be that much further away. She didn't seem to have good judgment when it came to men. Perhaps steering clear for a while was the best idea.

And while the occasional thought of *one day when I have kids* would pop up from time to time, that day never seemed to arrive. She still had plenty of childbearing years ahead of her, but it already seemed like a lost cause unless she got brave enough to buy sperm and go it alone. That would be a terrible decision. She'd never had a mother, so how would she know how to be one? The last thing she wanted to do was fail at something that important the way her mother had.

"I don't need a family of my own," Georgia argued. "I have you."

Sheila set her tea down on the coffee table and moved over to the couch beside Georgia. She put her arm around her shoulder and hugged her close. "Yes, you do. But you don't have to be in Detroit for that. You'll have me wherever you are, Georgia. I know you've had a lot of bad things happen all at once, but you can't just give up on everything you've worked for. You could always take the job at Elite Industries, couldn't you?"

That offer was technically still on the table. If she accepted the position, it would be minus the mistress part, of course. But even if she did feel like she'd had some kind of breakthrough with Sutton, he wouldn't be around long. She didn't know Eve well enough, and she wouldn't want her presumptions about their professional relationship to get her canned again in a few months. "I'm not sure that's a very good idea."

"Well, that's the beauty of a town like Chicago. There is nothing but opportunity there."

"You're right," Georgia agreed. She knew Sheila was right. It just seemed easier to run away than to deal with the mess she'd left behind. In Detroit, she'd never have to worry about running into Carson, and then maybe she could ignore the heartbreak. She felt the prickle of tears sting her eyes again.

"Are you going to be okay, Georgia?"

She shrugged as she looked at her only friend and fought back the tears. "You know, a part of me was always expecting my mother to do what she did. Whether I can blame her or her addiction, it just seemed like I was waiting for the other shoe to drop. The thing with Carson is that much harder. I thought what we had was… I don't know. The things he said to me were just so cruel, so unlike the man I knew. He lashed out at me like an abused dog."

"In that case, do you blame the dog or the owner that abused her?" Sheila asked.

"Carson is too old to blame anyone but himself. But I could tell that I'd hit his hot buttons. It caught me so off guard, you know? He's handsome, successful, rich, powerful…and yet he seemed to just be waiting for me to turn on him."

"Sometimes the more successful you are, the more people are waiting around to knock you off your pedestal. Everyone has their issues. His knee-jerk reflex was stronger than most, but it sounds like a pretty hard-wired defense mechanism. Here's a question for you, though. If he realizes he's made a mistake and apologizes, would you take him back?"

Georgia had pondered that question since she got to Detroit. "I probably would," she admitted. "I've given everyone else in my life a second chance, even when they didn't deserve it and I regretted it in the end. Maybe this time will be different. Or not. But either way, I love him. I might be a fool, but I do."

"Okay," Sheila said. "So when he has this miraculous revelation and rushes to tell you he's sorry and how much he loves you, how the heck is he supposed to find you here?"

The six potential and confirmed children of Sutton Winchester were gathered silently around the old man's conference room table. No one seemed very keen to chat; they just glared across the table at one another.

The middle sister, Nora, had come from Colorado today. Carson had never seen her before. Since she'd left Chicago, he didn't run into her at any industry events the way he tended to bump into Eve. She'd gotten out and he didn't blame her. She was probably the smartest one of them all.

A moment later, the door opened and Sutton came in with a woman at his side. Carson hoped it wasn't another mistress. His father didn't need any more women in his life, and he certainly didn't need to be flaunting one in front of his kids. Of course, she didn't really look like his type. This lady was very buttoned up, almost studious looking. She was wearing a light gray suit, and her wheat-blond hair was pulled back into a tight bun.

Sutton pulled back the chair for the woman to take the seat beside him, and he sat at the head of the table. Carson noted a slight tremble in the old man's hand as he moved. He did look thinner than the last time he'd seen him. Sutton looked like hell, frankly. Georgia had been right: this wasn't just a stomach bug.

"I'm sure that all of you are curious about why I called you here today," Sutton began. "If I had time to waste, I'd prolong the suspense, but I don't, so I'll get right to the point. I'm dying."

Carson didn't react. Instead he turned to watch

his three newfound sisters gasp in shock and horror. Nora's hand flew to cover her mouth, and Grace's eyes started to well up with tears.

"What?" Eve asked. "Dying? Are you sure?"

"Yes. This is Dr. Wilde," he said, gesturing to the prim woman beside him. "She'll be treating me at the Midwest Regional Medical Center for my stage IV lung cancer—not that there's much that can be done. We'll try a few things because I hate just lying down and letting cancer win, but I've already come to terms with the fact that I won't see the new year."

Stage IV. Cancer. Dead before the new year. The words flew around in Carson's brain as he tried to process it all. Finally he turned to Brooks, and they exchanged a meaningful glance. They'd gone into this thinking they had plenty of time to achieve their goals. Even if Sutton was stubborn, they knew they would eventually convince him to change his will and include them. But now…the clock was ticking. The father they'd just gained would be gone before they knew it.

"I'm getting things in order, and then I'll be going to the hospital. I'm not sure when I'll be discharged, if ever," he continued.

"We're going to be trying some experimental treatments," Dr. Wilde said. "At this point, we don't have anything to lose, and we have everything to gain. But really, all we're buying your father is time. Eventually he will succumb."

"Oh, Daddy!" Grace leaped up from her seat and rushed to give her father a hug.

Carson watched with a twinge of jealousy as Sutton gently stroked his daughter's hair and held her close. He doubted his father would ever hug him like that. They wouldn't get to that point even if Sutton had decades to live instead of months.

"Don't you worry about me, Gracie. I've lived three lifetimes while I've been on this earth."

"How am I going to handle all of this without you?" Eve said with a startled look in her eye. The pressure of taking over Elite Industries seemed to be weighing as heavily on her shoulders as the loss of her father.

"Oh, please, Eve," Sutton said with a dismissive tone. "You're smart and capable. You practically run the company now. You'll be fine. You will all be just fine without me. I think some of you might even be better off," Sutton said, pointedly looking at Carson.

It was the first time they'd made eye contact since the truth came out about Carson's paternity. The first hint of acknowledgment.

"All that said, we have some other business to tend to today." Sutton held up a package with a logo that Carson recognized from the lab. "It seems we've received the test results for Graham and Brooks. Would one of you care to do the honors?"

Brooks took the folder and quickly opened it. Carson just watched Sutton. There was a smugness on his face that convinced him that Sutton had been telling the truth all along. He didn't need the test results to know the twins weren't his children. But how could he know for certain?

"Sutton Winchester is not our father," Brooks said after scanning the document for what seemed like a lifetime.

Sutton sat back in his chair and folded his hands casually over his stomach. There was a small curl of amusement on his lips as he watched Graham and Brooks reel from the news.

Carson wasn't taking it well, either. He'd spent his whole life feeling different, feeling separated from his brothers. He'd convinced himself that it was just because they were twins and had an extraordinarily close relationship. He'd ignored the fact that he looked different. But now the variations were glaringly obvious.

It just left one question. If Sutton wasn't their father, then who the hell was? They were back at the drawing board with his brothers' paternity.

"Well," Graham said as he turned to Sutton, "now that this is settled, I believe we can move forward with the requested changes to the will."

"You don't still expect to be included, do you?" Eve asked.

"No," Graham said. "Since I am not your half brother, Brooks and I have no claim. But Carson still does. The only difference is that the estate should be divided by four instead of six."

"This is ridiculous!" one of the sisters shouted.

Carson didn't bother to look up and see which one it was. Everyone at the table started yelling all at once. He didn't bother to open his mouth. He let them carry on.

In that moment, none of it really mattered to him. Yes, he was still angry with his father, but it sounded like cancer would get his revenge faster and more thoroughly than Carson ever would. If he got any money out of the estate, he would put it toward the hospital along with the twenty million Sutton had already donated. The children's hospital built in his mother's name would be amazing.

And on the day it opened, there would be a different PR director by his side. It seemed wrong that any of it could happen without Georgia. She had been with him since—

The thought was interrupted as a sudden realization hit Carson like a punch to the gut.

She *knew*.

Georgia knew that Sutton was dying. He didn't know why Sutton had decided to tell her before he even told his own children, but it had to be the secret she couldn't share. In an instant, all the pieces of that horrible evening started to fit together. That's why she was encouraging him to get to know his fa-

ther, damn near pushing him into it. She knew that
he wouldn't have much time with Sutton.

And perhaps his pending mortality was why Sutton had written such a big check to the foundation. It
wasn't as though he could take it with him, despite
his best efforts. Was it possible it had nothing to do
with Georgia's relationship with Sutton at all?

As quickly as it all came together, a final thought
entered Carson's mind—he was a royal jerk. He'd
accused her of taking sides, being disloyal to the
company and to him, and even suggested she'd been
sleeping with Sutton. All this after he'd encouraged
her to keep seeing Sutton so Carson could use her
for information.

Without thinking, Carson stood suddenly. The
whole table stopped squabbling and looked at him
in anticipation.

"I have to go."

Graham reached out and grabbed his arm. "What
do you mean, you have to go?"

"I've got to find Georgia and apologize."

Both twins looked at him with aqua eyes that reflected their concern that he'd gone mad. "We're
kind of in the middle of something important. Do
you have to go right now?" Brooks asked.

"Absolutely, right now," Sutton agreed, backing
him up in a way Carson hadn't expected. "Don't let
a jewel like that get away, son." He winked and gave
him a small smile.

Son? A lump formed in Carson's throat. He couldn't respond to his brothers or his father. He knew he just had to get out of there. Without another word, he stepped away from the table and made his way out of the office. He had more important issues to tend to.

He had to track Georgia down.

Thirteen

Carson blew into the Newport building like a tornado. The elevator couldn't move fast enough for him as it raced to the top floor, where their executive offices were.

"Rebecca!" he shouted almost the moment the doors started to part. "Rebecca, I need you!"

By the time he reached his assistant's desk outside his office, Rebecca's eyes were wide with surprise and panic. "What is it, sir? Is everything okay?"

"Yes and no," he said, making a beeline for his door. "Please come in and bring your tablet."

He settled in at his desk and turned to face Rebecca, who was at the ready, as always. "I need you to help me find Georgia."

"She's not in today, Mr. Newport. I actually haven't seen her this week."

"Yes, I know. That's because she quit."

"Oh no," she gasped. "When? I hadn't heard anything about it."

"A few days ago."

Rebecca studied him for a moment. "What did you do, sir?"

Carson looked up in surprise. She'd been his assistant for five years now. Apparently she knew him better than he gave her credit for. "Well, you know we were dating, right?"

"Everyone knew, sir."

"Okay, then. As expected, I put my foot so far into my mouth, I crapped my shoe. It's all my fault, and I know it. I'm not sure she'll ever forgive me for being such a jerk, but I'm going to try."

"Are you in love with her?"

He'd never really had a personal conversation like this with Rebecca. Typically their discussions were work related, or they exchanged casual pleasantries about her kids and how her weekend was. They usually didn't talk about Carson's personal life. Of course, Carson hadn't really had much of a personal life until recently. At a time like this, he needed all the help he could get, especially if it came in the form of feminine relationship wisdom.

Did he love her? "Yes. Absolutely." He knew that much was true when Georgia's presumed betrayal had hurt so badly. He'd let himself fall for her only to have her drop him for a bigger fish just like Candy had, only this one hurt ten times worse because he loved her. Realizing she hadn't done any of the things he'd accused her of only made it that much more painful.

"That's refreshing to hear," Rebecca said. "Does she love you?"

That he wasn't sure about. Because of her tears and anger, he was certain his accusations cut deep. She'd never said she was in love with him, but it was early. No one wanted to be first. To get her back, he would shout it from the rooftops. "I don't know. I hope so."

Rebecca nodded thoughtfully. "And what big gesture are you planning to woo her back?"

Big gesture? "I haven't really thought that far yet. First we've got to find her."

"We'll find her, sir. I have no worries about that. But when we do, it's crucial you know what you're going to say. Screw that up and we might as well save ourselves the time of tracking her down."

Carson swallowed hard. She was right. This was one of the most important things he would ever do, and he couldn't wing it. Georgia deserved better. "What do you suggest?"

"For one, apologize. No caveats, no justifications. Just apologize. Two, give her flowers. It's a cliché, but that's because it works. My husband can make me absolutely insane and then walk in with a handful of lilies and I melt. Do you know what kind she likes?"

"No."

Rebecca twisted her lips in thought. "When you get to the florist, pick some that remind you of her. You can't go wrong with that tactic. Then tell her you love her and see what happens. From there, it's up to her."

"That's it?" That sounded far too easy.

"Well, it depends." Rebecca arched a curious eyebrow at him before she laid down her challenge. "Are you wanting to go all the way? Pull out all the stops?"

Yes. Yes, he did want to go all the way, and he knew exactly where to take it from there. "You're right. All the way it is. I'll take care of that part this afternoon. Now we've got to get her back, you and I. The problem is, she's vanished. We've got to figure out where she's gone. I just went by her building and her doorman says she's got a hold on her mail with no expected return date. That's not a good sign."

"Does she have family nearby or friends she would stay with?"

"I don't think so, at least not family. I'm not so sure about friends."

"Would you like me to look in her office? Maybe she had an address book or something? I could also get the IT department to log into her laptop, and we can see who's in her contact lists."

Alarm bells started going off in Carson's head.

Yes, that was probably the smartest, most direct choice, but he remembered the look in Georgia's eyes when she realized he's looked into her purse. She had very strong personal boundaries, and understandably so. Technically her office was company property and he could do what he liked, especially since she'd quit, but if he could avoid that, he wanted to.

"Let's start with talking to her assistant and co-workers first to see if they have any ideas. Maybe we can strike gold without digging too far into her personal things. I know she doesn't like that. Let me know the minute you find anything."

Rebecca stood up, tapping at her screen. She was almost to the door when a name popped into Carson's mind.

"Rebecca? Let me know if you find any references to a Sheila. That's the only person she's ever mentioned. She probably lives, or at least lived, in Detroit."

"Sheila. Got it." With that, she disappeared to start the hunt.

With her on Georgia's trail, Carson started on the next task—going all the way. He called to make an appointment at Tiffany and Co. and headed there about an hour later. By the time he returned to the office with a tiny blue bag and a stomach full of nerves, Rebecca was sitting at her desk with a bright smile. "What?"

She handed over a piece of paper with a name, a phone number and a Detroit address for Sheila.

"Georgia's assistant had this information. Apparently she sent flowers to her on Mother's Day. That sounds like the place to start."

"You're amazing," Carson said with a wide grin. "I'm going to give her a call right now."

Carson went into his office and shut the door. He had a feeling that Sheila would know where Georgia had run off to. He'd follow her anywhere she'd gone. He just needed to know what flight to take.

The phone rang for what felt like a lifetime. "Hello?" a woman's voice finally answered.

"Hello. Is this Sheila?"

"Yes, it is. Who's this?"

"My name is Carson Newport. I'm—"

"Hold on a second," Sheila said, interrupting him. He sat waiting silently, his heart pounding in his throat as he heard her shuffling around and then doing something that sounded like closing a door. "Okay, that's better. I don't want her to hear us talking."

Her? "Is Georgia there with you?"

"She is. She's been here a few days."

He'd hit the jackpot on the first try. *Thank you, Rebecca.* She was getting a raise. "Thank goodness," he said. "I didn't know where else to look if you didn't know where she'd gone. I've got to get her back."

"I'm glad to hear that. She doesn't have many places to go, Carson. Georgia never really had a home or a family. I'm just her social worker, but I'm the only person she has. Except for you. Does she still have you?"

"Yes, she absolutely still has me. I don't want her to ever feel like she has to run away. I want her to run *to* me from here on out."

"You sound very confident, Carson, but Georgia is very hurt. You crossed a line with her. She's not the kind that trusts easily to begin with, so it's going to take a lot more than a smile and a casual 'I'm sorry' to earn her trust back."

"I know that. She deserves far more than that," Carson answered. "She deserves a man she can trust. One who makes her feel safe and loved, and I want to be that man. I love her and I feel like a fool for letting my past issues color the situation. I—"

"Honey, save it for her," Sheila interrupted. "How soon can you get to Detroit?"

Carson looked down at his watch. It wasn't a long flight, but the logistics of the airport, even with a private flight, would take time. "By dinnertime."

"Good. I'll keep her distracted and at the house until you get here. She was talking about going out to eat, but I'm going to insist on cooking something special that she can't refuse. You've got my address on Mayflower?"

The slip of paper showed the right address. "I do. I'll have a car take me straight there from the airport."

"Good. I look forward to meeting you, Carson."

He hung up the phone, feeling a triumphant surge of adrenaline running through his veins. "Rebecca, book me the next available flight to Detroit!" he shouted and started gathering up everything he needed to leave.

When he looked up a few minutes later, Brooks was standing in the doorway with a frown on his face. His large frame filled the space; he was like an angry Viking. Carson was about to get it, he was certain. With Georgia absorbing his every thought, he'd forgotten that he'd left his brothers in the lion's den that morning.

"What the hell was all that about back at Sutton's? You walked out of a huge meeting. You left Graham and me dangling after the paternity test bombshell."

"I'm sorry," Carson said. He hadn't really considered that his brothers were probably upset about the news that their father was still a mystery. Graham had barely blinked, launching into an argument that would just secure a larger piece of the pie for Carson. "How did it go?"

Brooks shrugged. "A stalemate. With him dying, we don't have much time. And of course, there's still the matter of tracking down our father. How could you leave in the middle of all that? It was a crucial turning point for our plan."

Carson knew that, but in the moment, it simply hadn't mattered. "I just had to go. This was more important."

He didn't think it was possible, but Brooks's frown deepened. "She's just a woman, Carson. They come and go. We're talking about getting revenge for our mother. Making Sutton pay for how he treated her and abandoned you. How can some lady you're dating possibly be more important?"

Carson took a deep breath and sighed. Nothing he said would diffuse his brother's anger. It had taken Carson a while to get to this point, too. "Nothing we do to Sutton is going to change what happened to Mom. We can't change the past. We can't right the wrongs of thirty years ago. I've decided the future—my future with Georgia—is more important." He stood up and grabbed the baby blue bag from his desktop. "And she's not just a lady I'm dating, Brooks. At least, not for much longer."

"Is that what I think it is?" Brooks asked, his aqua eyes wide with surprise.

"Yep. The future starts today."

Georgia was helping put together a salad when a knock sounded at the front door. Sheila had dismissed her offer of a nice dinner out as a thank-you for taking her in, so she insisted on at least helping to cook.

"I'm in the middle of finishing up the pasta," Sheila said. "Can you get the door? It's probably just a package. I'm addicted to Amazon Prime."

"Sure thing." Georgia wiped her hands on a dish

towel and trotted over to the front door. She flung it open, and stood frozen in shock when she found Carson on the doorstep instead of the delivery man.

"Hello, Georgia." He was wearing one of his best Armani suits and holding a bundle of bright pinkish-red roses in his hands.

How had he found her here? Georgia's gaze narrowed in suspicion as she glanced over her shoulder. The kitchen was miraculously empty, confirming what she thought to be true. Sheila had conspired against her and brought him here. She'd given Georgia no warning at all. She could've at least told her to change. Her hair was in a ponytail. She was wearing a pair of capri jeans and an oversized Detroit Lions T-shirt she'd bought at Walmart because she hadn't brought any clothes with her. She self-consciously ran her hand over her hair to smooth the flyaways.

"Are you going to say something?" he asked. His green eyes were pleading with her.

She wasn't going to give in that easily. She wanted to. Seeing him in that suit with those sad green eyes made her want to melt to the floor, but she wouldn't. Carson had a lot of groveling to do before she was going to forgive him for how he'd treated her. "I would, but it seems that everything I say or do is twisted and used against me somehow. It's probably better that I just let you do all the talking."

Carson nodded, his gaze dropping to the flowers in his hands. "That's fair. I deserve that. You're absolutely right. I took your well-intended advice and hard work for the company and turned them into something licentious. I should've trusted you the way you asked me to, and I didn't. I am very sorry for that. I realize now that I colored everything with my own hang-ups, and they had nothing to do with you. You didn't deserve any of the horrible things I said to you that night."

Georgia listened to him as he spilled his guts. He seemed genuine in his apology. But that wasn't nearly enough to heal what he'd broken.

"Sutton got everyone together yesterday and announced that he's dying. Of course, you already knew that." Carson looked at her, probably searching for some confirmation in her eyes. She kept a neutral expression. "I'm not sure he and I will ever be close, but I understand now what you meant about giving it a shot while I have the chance. We're far from good, but I'm open to the possibility, at least. That's a big step for me."

"Good for you. What about your brothers?" she asked in a flat tone. It would be hard for Carson to accept his father if his brothers felt different.

"Well, it turns out they're just my half brothers. Sutton is not their father."

Georgia nodded. This was also not news to her. She'd been right when she said Sutton was a jerk, but not a liar. "He told them that, but Graham wouldn't listen."

"I'm sure he did. Listen, I'm not sure what's going to happen with Sutton, or my brothers, or anything else there, but I know that I want you back in Chicago when it happens. The Newport Corporation needs you, Georgia. The plans for the charity gala have fallen apart since you left. The donation from Sutton needs to be put to good use and frankly, I need help. You're an integral part of the Newport family, and we need you. I want you there when we have the ribbon cutting because this only could've happened with you at my side."

Georgia felt her hopes start to crumble. Was that all he wanted from her? Public relations skills? He'd wasted a trip if that was all he had to offer her. "You've come an awfully long way just to offer me my job back, Carson. You could've done that over the phone." Not that she would've answered.

He winced slightly and shook his head. "No, I couldn't. And you know full well this is about more than just your job, Georgia."

"Then what *is* it about? Because that's all you've talked about."

"Okay. I know. Work is just easier to talk about for me." Carson swallowed hard and thrust the roses out to her. "These are for you. They're American Beauties. I thought that was the perfect rose for you."

She accepted the bundle of flowers and brought them up to her nose. They were amazingly fragrant and delicate with velvety petals. No one had ever given her flowers before. She hadn't even gotten a corsage at the prom because she didn't go. She never could've afforded the dress and everything that went with it. Since then, her relationships had been far too casual for a romantic gesture like flowers.

"Thank you," she said, unable to tear her eyes away from them.

"What I really came here to say…aside from apologizing…is that I miss you so much. Once you left, it was like I had this hole in my chest that I couldn't fill. I've always felt that way about not having my father in my life, like there was a part of me missing somehow. I'm sure you know how that feels, too, growing up without any family.

"After our fight," he continued, "I realized that those two feelings were different. In reality, I couldn't control my father and if he wanted to be in my life or not. But I was the reason you were gone, and I could do something about it. Blood doesn't always make a family. Sometimes it's more about who you choose. I don't just want you to be a part of the Newport Corporation family, Georgia. I want you to be a part of my family. We've both felt like we haven't really ever had one, or that we've lost it along the way. What I'm offering you is the chance to have a family, a real family, at last. With me."

Georgia clutched the roses in her hands as he spoke. Her chest grew tighter with every word. Was he really saying what it sounded like? That was impossible.

"I love you, Georgia. I'm stubborn and stupid and scared to death of this, and I know that I almost ruined it…maybe I have…but it doesn't change how I feel for you. I've spent my life being afraid of losing people because I wasn't worthy of their love. When I thought the same thing was happening with you, I reacted. I exploded. I pushed you away to protect myself, and it was absolutely the wrong thing to do.

"In the end, I was just as alone, just as heartbroken as if you'd left me, but I did it to myself. I don't want to make that same mistake twice. So this time," Carson said as he reached into his pocket, "I'm going to make it permanent."

When Carson pulled his hand from his inner breast pocket, there was a small, distinctively aquacolored box in his hand. A Tiffany and Co. jewelry box by the looks of it. No one had ever given her jewelry, either, and since her mother had cleaned her out, the contents of that box were all the jewelry in the world that was hers. Or might be hers.

Georgia watched as Carson sank down onto one knee on Sheila's doorstep. "Georgia, I want us to start our own family here and now. You and me. I want us to put the past and all our pain behind us and start our lives together anew. If you'll agree to be my wife, I promise to do everything I can to make you feel loved, valued, safe and special every day for the rest of your life."

Carson took the lid off the box to reveal a classic round Tiffany solitaire in a platinum band. She was no expert, but it had to be at least two or three carats. "I hope you like it. I wanted to go with something classic and traditional since neither of us have had much of that in our lives. You're beautiful and timeless and I wanted your ring to be the same."

"It's gorgeous," she said, although her words were muffled by her hand covering her mouth.

"Will you marry me, Georgia?" Carson held up the ring between his fingertips. The sunlight caught the large gem, and it sparkled with a thousand colors.

"Say yes, you fool!" a voice whispered harshly from the back of the house.

She didn't need Sheila's prompting to make up her mind. "Yes," she said, tossing the flowers onto the nearby table. "Not just yes, but hell yes."

Carson grinned wide and slipped the ring onto her finger. Squeezing her hand in his, he stood up and looked down at her with eyes that reflected the love and adoration she'd never expected to see. "I'm pleased by your enthusiasm," he said.

"You ain't seen nothing yet." Georgia smiled, wrapping her arms around his neck and bringing her lips to his.

* * * * *

Don't miss a single installment of the
DYNASTIES: THE NEWPORTS
*Passion and chaos consume a Chicago
real estate empire*

SAYING YES TO THE BOSS
by Andrea Laurence

AN HEIR FOR THE BILLIONAIRE
by Kat Cantrell

CLAIMED BY THE COWBOY
by Sarah M. Anderson

HIS SECRET BABY BOMBSHELL
by Jules Bennett

BACK IN THE ENEMY'S BED
by Michelle Celmer

THE TEXAN'S ONE NIGHT STAND-OFF
by Charlene Sands

Available now from Harlequin Desire!

***

*If you're on Twitter, tell us what you think
of Harlequin Desire! #harlequindesire*

COMING NEXT MONTH FROM

HARLEQUIN® Desire

Available August 9, 2016

#2461 FOR BABY'S SAKE
Billionaires and Babies • by Janice Maynard
Lila Baxter is all business. That's why she and easygoing
James Kavanagh broke off their relationship. But when she
unexpectedly inherits a baby, she'll have to face him again...and he
might win it all this time.

#2462 AN HEIR FOR THE BILLIONAIRE
Dynasties: The Newports • by Kat Cantrell
When single mother Nora O'Malley stumbles into the reclusive life of
her childhood best friend, he'll have to confront his dark past, and put
love before business, if he's ever to find happiness with her little family...

#2463 PREGNANT BY THE MAVERICK MILLIONAIRE
From Mavericks to Married • by Joss Wood
When former hockey player turned team CEO finds out his fling with a
determinedly single matchmaker has led to unexpected consequences,
he insists he'll be part of her life from now on...for the baby's sake, of
course!

#2464 CONTRACT WEDDING, EXPECTANT BRIDE
Courtesan Brides • by Yvonne Lindsay
If King Rocco does not have a bride and heir in a year's time, an ancient
law will force him to relinquish all power to the enemy. Courtesan
Ottavia Romolo might be the solution, but she demands his heart, too...

#2465 THE CEO DADDY NEXT DOOR
by Karen Booth
CEO and single father Marcus Chambers will only date women who
would be suitable mothers for his young daughter, but when his
free-spirited neighbor temporarily moves in after a fire destroys her
apartment, he finds himself falling for the worst possible candidate!

#2466 WAKING UP WITH THE BOSS
by Sheri WhiteFeather
Billionaire playboy Jake expected the fling with his personal assistant,
Carol, to be one and done. But when a surprise pregnancy brings them
closer, will it make this all-business boss want more than the bottom
line?

**YOU CAN FIND MORE INFORMATION ON UPCOMING HARLEQUIN® TITLES,
FREE EXCERPTS AND MORE AT WWW.HARLEQUIN.COM.**

HDCNM0716

REQUEST YOUR FREE BOOKS!
2 FREE NOVELS PLUS 2 FREE GIFTS!

HARLEQUIN®

Desire

ALWAYS POWERFUL, PASSIONATE AND PROVOCATIVE

YES! Please send me 2 FREE Harlequin® Desire novels and my 2 FREE gifts (gifts are worth about $10). After receiving them, if I don't wish to receive any more books, I can return the shipping statement marked "cancel." If I don't cancel, I will receive 6 brand-new novels every month and be billed just $4.55 per book in the U.S. or $5.24 per book in Canada. That's a savings of at least 13% off the cover price! It's quite a bargain! Shipping and handling is just 50¢ per book in the U.S. and 75¢ per book in Canada.* I understand that accepting the 2 free books and gifts places me under no obligation to buy anything. I can always return a shipment and cancel at any time. Even if I never buy another book, the two free books and gifts are mine to keep forever.

225/326 HDN GH2P

Name   (PLEASE PRINT)

Address   Apt. #

City   State/Prov.   Zip/Postal Code

Signature (if under 18, a parent or guardian must sign)

Mail to the **Reader Service:**
IN U.S.A.: P.O. Box 1867, Buffalo, NY 14240-1867
IN CANADA: P.O. Box 609, Fort Erie, Ontario L2A 5X3

Want to try two free books from another line?
Call 1-800-873-8635 or visit www.ReaderService.com.

* Terms and prices subject to change without notice. Prices do not include applicable taxes. Sales tax applicable in N.Y. Canadian residents will be charged applicable taxes. Offer not valid in Quebec. This offer is limited to one order per household. Not valid for current subscribers to Harlequin Desire books. All orders subject to credit approval. Credit or debit balances in a customer's account(s) may be offset by any other outstanding balance owed by or to the customer. Please allow 4 to 6 weeks for delivery. Offer available while quantities last.

Your Privacy—The Reader Service is committed to protecting your privacy. Our Privacy Policy is available online at www.ReaderService.com or upon request from the Reader Service.

We make a portion of our mailing list available to reputable third parties that offer products we believe may interest you. If you prefer that we not exchange your name with third parties, or if you wish to clarify or modify your communication preferences, please visit us at www.ReaderService.com/consumerschoice or write to us at Reader Service Preference Service, P.O. Box 9062, Buffalo, NY 14240-9062. Include your complete name and address.

HDI5

SPECIAL EXCERPT FROM

HARLEQUIN™

Desire

*Lila Baxter is all business. That's why she and easygoing
James Kavanagh broke off their relationship. But when
she unexpectedly inherits a baby, she'll have to face him
again…and he might win it all this time.*

*Read on for a sneak peek of
FOR BABY'S SAKE, the latest installment in the
KAVANAGHS OF SILVER GLEN series
by USA TODAY bestselling author*
Janice Maynard.

James Kavanagh liked working with his hands. Unlike his
eldest brother, Liam, who spent his days wearing an Italian
tailored suit, James was most comfortable in old jeans
and T-shirts. Truth be told, it was a good disguise. No one
expected a rich man to look like a guy who labored for a
paycheck.

That was fine with James. He didn't need people sucking
up to him because he was a Kavanagh. He wanted to be
judged on his own merits.

At the end of the day, a man was only as rich as his
reputation.

As he dipped his paintbrush into the can balanced on the
top of the ladder, he saw movement at the house next door.
Lila's house. A house he'd once known all too well.

It didn't matter. He was over her. Completely. The two of
them had been a fire that burned hot and bright, leaving only
ashes. It was for the best. Lila was too uptight, too driven,
too everything.

Still, something was going on. Lila's silver Subaru was parked in its usual spot. But it was far too early for her to be arriving home from work. He gave up the pretense of painting and watched as she got out of the car.

She was tall and curvy and had long blond curls that no amount of hair spray could tame. Lila had the body of a pinup girl and the brains of an accountant, a lethal combo. Then came his second clue that things were out of kilter. Lila was wearing jeans and a windbreaker. On a Monday.

He could have ignored all of that. Honestly, he was fine with the status quo. Lila had her job as vice president of the local bank, and James had the pleasure of dating women who were uncomplicated.

As he watched, Lila closed the driver's door and opened the door to the backseat. Leaning in, she gave him a tantalizing view of a nicely rounded ass. He'd always had a thing for butts. Lila's was first-class.

Suddenly, all thoughts of butts and sex and his long-ago love affair with his frustrating neighbor flew out the window. Because when Lila straightened, she was holding a baby.

Don't miss FOR BABY'S SAKE
by USA TODAY bestselling author Janice Maynard.
Available August 2016!

And meet all the Kavanagh brothers in the
***KAVANAGHS OF SILVER GLEN** series—*
In the mountains of North Carolina, one family discovers
that wealth means nothing without love.

A NOT-SO-INNOCENT SEDUCTION
BABY FOR KEEPS
CHRISTMAS IN THE BILLIONAIRE'S BED
TWINS ON THE WAY
SECOND CHANCE WITH THE BILLIONAIRE
HOW TO SLEEP WITH THE BOSS
FOR BABY'S SAKE

www.Harlequin.com

Copyright © 2016 by Janice Maynard

HDEXP0716

Whatever You're Into… Passionate Reads

Looking for more passionate reads from Harlequin®?
Fear not! Harlequin® Presents, Harlequin® Desire and
Harlequin® Blaze offer you irresistible romance stories
featuring powerful heroes.

HARLEQUIN *Presents*

Do you want alpha males, decadent glamour and jet-set
lifestyles? Step into the sensational, sophisticated world of
Harlequin® Presents, where sinfully tempting heroes ignite a
fierce and wickedly irresistible passion!

HARLEQUIN *Desire*

Harlequin® Desire novels are powerful, passionate and
provocative contemporary romances set against a backdrop of
wealth, privilege and sweeping family saga. Alpha heroes with
a soft side meet strong-willed but vulnerable heroines amid a
dramatic world of divided loyalties, high-stakes conflict and
intense emotion.

HARLEQUIN *Blaze*

Harlequin® Blaze stories sizzle with strong heroines and
irresistible heroes playing the game of modern love and lust.
They're fun, sexy and always steamy.

Be sure to check out our full selection of books
within each series every month!

www.Harlequin.com

HPASSION2016

Turn your love of reading into rewards you'll love with
Harlequin My Rewards

**Join for FREE today at
www.HarlequinMyRewards.com**

Earn **FREE BOOKS** of your choice.

Experience **EXCLUSIVE OFFERS** and contests.

Enjoy **BOOK RECOMMENDATIONS**
selected just for you.

PLUS! Sign up now
and get **500** points
right away!

Earn
FREE
REWARDS
Join
Today!
HarlequinMyRewards.com

MYR16R

Love the Harlequin book you just read?

Your opinion matters.

Review this book on your favorite book site, review site, blog or your own social media properties and share your opinion with other readers!

Be sure to connect with us at:
Harlequin.com/Newsletters
Facebook.com/HarlequinBooks
Twitter.com/HarlequinBooks

HREVIEWS